AFTER HOURS

DARA GIRARD

ILORI
Press Books, LLC

ISBN: 978-1949764482

AFTER HOURS

Published by ILORI Press Books

This is a work of fiction. Names, characters, places and incidents are either the product of the author's imagination or are used fictitiously, and any resemblance to actual persons, living or dead is entirely coincidental.

ILORI PRESS BOOKS, LLC

P.O. Box 10332

Silver Spring, MD 20914

www.iloripressbooks.com

Henson Series

Table for Two

Gaining Interest

Careless Rapture

Dangerous Curves

Familiar Stranger

It Happened One Wedding

Unexpected Pleasure

Midnight Promise

Sweet Temptation

Always and Forever

Truly Yours

Say Yes

Clifton Sisters

The Sapphire Pendant

The Amber Stone

The Emerald Ring

Fortune Brothers

A Tempting Proposal

A Seductive Arrangement

An Unforgettable Moment

Novels

Honest Betrayal

The Daughters of Winston Barnett

Remember My Name

Illusive Flame

Winterwood Lane

Promise Me

This Changes Everything

Sparks

Benjamin Marshall Bishop was a class-A bastard. But that didn't surprise anyone, considering his father had been an even bigger one. At seventy-three, he'd lived a decade longer than his father, although many had wished for an earlier demise, and now he was close enough to the grave for people to wish that destiny would give him a little--or rather a hard-- push. He ruled his empire from inside his mansion, which sat isolated on twenty-two acres of land like a ghoulish gargoyle. He rarely left his sick bed, wheezing through an oxygen mask, fighting the cancer that many hoped would drag him straight down to the underworld.

But Bishop was a determined man and planned to live a lot longer than his doctors predicted; not just through his business but through his only son.

Curtis Bishop was the spitting image of his father, tall and dark, with ruggedly handsome features and a temperament so cold, people whispered that icicles grew on his tongue and birds stopped singing when he passed, as though a chill, ominous wind had blown past. So, when he suddenly appeared that Monday morning, after the Thanksgiving holiday, and stood high above the factory floor casting his gaze over the workers, terror rippled throughout the factory. Located in Pikesville, a small town outside of Philadelphia, the Valdan factory made specialized garments for the fashion industry. Curtis' presence there was about as welcomed as an oil slick in an ocean. And just as a prey knows when a predator is approaching, the hum of machines grew ever more anxious.

His piercing dark eyes, unsmiling mouth, and unyielding countenance betrayed no emotion away as his gaze swept over the room. He lifted his arm and the room grew totally silent, as though he had the power of a magician able to cast a spell. A worker, standing nearby, handed him a microphone. Curtis ignored him. The worker got the message and put the microphone away. Curtis made it clear he expected complete attention and obedience.

"It is with great regret that I must inform you that this factory will close at the end of the year," he said, with no trace of regret or apology in his tone. "Thank you for your service. You will all receive a bonus in your final paycheck for this inconvenience."

The mention of the word 'inconvenience' seemed to be an obligatory addition and no one felt it was genuine. The devastating announcement swept over the factory floor, but no one dared make a sound, although the thought of lost wages and security pierced the hearts of everyone present.

"That's all," he said, then nodded as a signal that time was money and he expected them to make him some.

After several seconds, the hum of the machines began again, but the tension in the air hung as thick as fog.

"Is it absolutely necessary?" Bill Homer, the plant manager said, gathering up a courage he didn't know he had. He was a short, middle-aged man, with thick eyebrows and a balding head, who still had the sharp gaze and quick movements of the physician he used to be. He knew that no one questioned a Bishop after a decision had been made, but he couldn't help think of the welfare of his workers and how the small Pennsylvania town would survive without the factory. Plus, he had a family of his own and news like this would devastate them, especially during the holidays. "Valdan has always hit its quotas. I've been able to recruit some of the finest workers in the region. Isn't there anything we can do?"

Curtis looked straight ahead and continued walking towards the exit.

Bill shifted his gaze to Curtis' executive assistant, Amera Thurston, hoping she had some influence. She wasn't much to look at. He wouldn't say she was plain, just non-descript, except for her light brown hair and eyes that made a striking contrast to her medium dark brown skin. Whenever he saw her, she reminded him of a wooden ruler--rigid and unyielding, but useful. He knew she would have to be, to stand in the presence of and work closely with the younger Bishop for as long as she had. Most of his executive assistants rarely lasted long. He didn't know much about her, other than that she was an immigrant who came to America from some small African country and kept mostly to herself.

She met his gaze, and to his surprise gave him a small nod of assurance. It wasn't much, but it was like a crumb to a starving man and he grasped it. Perhaps she could help make Bishop see reason, and give Valdan a second chance.

"May I have two minutes, sir?" she asked, or rather said, since there was no note of inquiry in her tone. She held back, while he continued walking. As Bishop's shadow, she rarely spoke, the sound of her voice always coming as a surprise. It was deeper than expected, and melodic. English clearly wasn't her first language, but she spoke it with an excellent command.

Curtis sent her a cool assessing glance, and Bill could feel the air chill around him. "One," he said. Bill half expected to see the frost of his breath hang in the air. He sent Bill an inscrutable look then left.

Bill released a long breath once Curtis was out of hearing. "Ms. Thurston, is there any way you can talk to him?"

"I'm sorry. I didn't know. If I had, I would have warned you."

The pain in her gaze brought tears to his eyes. Her unexpected compassion increased his sadness. She owed them nothing and yet she spoke as if she did. "He's worse than his father. I thought maybe he'd be different. How can he give people news like this during the holiday season?"

"The holidays don't exist for him. It's just about the money and I have a feeling this is what his father wants." She glanced around the factory and for a moment he thought he saw tears, but they quickly disappeared. "I don't have much influence, but I'll see what I can do." She dug into her handbag. "But that's not why I wanted to talk to you." She held out a small jar to him. "Here's some ointment for your son."

Bill took the jar from her, oddly touched. He remembered briefly complaining about his son's skin sensitivities and the expensive visits to the dermatologist that hadn't helped. He hadn't thought she'd paid any attention, although she always took time to ask him how his family was doing. He gripped the jar in his hand. At that moment her kind gesture made her look pretty to him, momentarily helping him forget the dire job market and his concern about how he would support his family before his savings ran out. "Thank you," he said. "Happy holidays."

She squeezed his arm then left.

Amera hurried to the waiting car, briefly inhaling the crisp autumn air, and the fresh scent of evergreens standing tall in the distance, blinking back the tears that stung her eyes. The town, only an hour away from headquarters in downtown Philadelphia, would struggle without the factory's life blood. The shock of Curtis' words had hit her like a bullet train. She'd secretly helped Bill get the position of plant manager, determined to repay a kind gesture he'd offered years ago. He'd saved lives and she wanted to save his. He didn't remember her, but that was no surprise, most people didn't. She hadn't been remarkable, but his generosity although brief, had carried her through her life. She'd followed his career when he'd stopped practicing medicine due to burnout and fallen on hard times after a major illness and a divorce. He'd remarried and settled in Pennsylvania and she'd decided to settle there too, always wondering how she could be the hero he'd briefly been to her. When she'd heard about a position opening up at Valdan, she'd anonymously sent information to him, then worked with HR to make sure he got the position. She'd been thrilled to hear how his family thrived, remembering that as a child she'd once wanted to be part of it, and glad that she could help. But now, that life was threatened again. She worried that Bill wouldn't be able to weather another job loss at his age and in such a tight market. She knew he had a son in graduate school and another with special needs. She had to find a way to help him.

"What took you so long?" Curtis asked as Amera settled in next to him in the back seat of the car, adjusting her bulky winter coat.

"I didn't go over a minute, sir," she said, buckling her seatbelt as the driver pulled from the parking space.

"What did he say?"

Amera rested her arm on the door and waited,

knowing he'd come to the conclusion on his own.

"The people are upset?"

"Hmm," she said giving him a noncommittal sound. She'd learned early not to be too chatty and wisely kept her feelings to herself.

Curtis sniffed and wiped his nose then swore.

She turned to him and saw the blood on his hand and quickly got the handy package of tissues she always kept nearby. She dutifully handed it to him. His nosebleeds were the only thing that made him human to her. After working with him for five years, she'd learned that they always came whenever he experienced a moment of tension or great emotional strain. He'd never admit it. He'd tried to pretend that they were just an annoying biological defect, but she knew there was something more psychological. As much as he wanted to be as distant and unfeeling as his father, something inside him rebelled. She knew it was the price he paid for being a bastard. But she knew she couldn't tell him so *and* keep her job. She clicked the car's back panel audio device then selected some classical music, knowing it would calm his nerves.

She hadn't expected her position as his executive assistant to last as long as it had. Seven others had held the position over the past twelve years, all dismissed or quitting within a matter of months. Strangely, she hadn't found the job that difficult. After growing up in two crowded orphanages and being in a refugee camp in a war torn land, she knew resilience and strife, and could take his mercurial moods and short temper. She was the one who paid attention to details. She kept his life orderly and, when necessary, smoothed his rough edges. But, truth be told, it was his money that made soothing ruffled feathers easiest.

"The factory is one of the best the company has," she said, trying to sound disinterested, although the thought of Valdan closing made her want to punch something, preferably him.

"We want to go in another direction."

"You mean your father."

Curtis sniffed, threw the tissue away in the small garbage bag off to the side, and reached for another, but the bleeding didn't stop.

Amera looked at him annoyed. If he stained his shirt, she'd have to send it to the cleaners and she wasn't in the mood. She handed him two more tissues. "Hold your nose and breathe calmly."

He sent her a look that could have withered a rose, but she only blinked back bored. She was not afraid of him.

"Did you get a chance to look at the proposal from the Peale House?" she asked, hoping to use a moment of weakness to catch his interest. Every year his company scrambled to find a charity to throw money at to use for a tax break.

"Shred it," he said in a nasal voice as he held his nose.

Amera gripped her hands then flexed them, keeping her voice calm. "I'm sorry?"

"Or recycle it, if you prefer. That's the tree hugging way to go, right?"

"That's not funny."

"When have I ever tried to be funny?"

"Did you even read it?" she asked fighting to keep her tone neutral. He didn't know that she was the one behind it. "I--I mean--they--spent days creating that and--"

"I don't give a damn how long they spent, they're not saying anything new and--"

"The bleeding has stopped," she cut in, staring at the ceiling and counting to ten.

"What?"

"The bleeding. It's stopped," she repeated, glancing at him then out the window.

Curtis looked down and grabbed another tissue just to make sure. Satisfied that she was correct, he threw the rest of the tissues away and sat back against the plush, black seats. "You're a smart woman, I'm surprised they got to you."

She turned to him. "Got to me?"

"Yes, the sob stories. Those people lay it on thicker during the holidays."

"*Those* people?"

He nodded, indifferent to the icy chill of her tone. "But the song is the same. Show your weakness and people will take advantage of you. They come to me every year with the same lame project."

"It's not lame. They focus on children and housing and-- ."

"You're missing the big picture. People think that just by putting an orphan in the picture makes something worthwhile. We've got free schools, free lunches, service programs all aimed at that population. Where has it gotten us? A lot of kids who feel the world now owes them a job and a good living. Hard work is the way to instill discipline and character. Not spoon feeding. They can use their adversity to make them strong."

"That sounds great in theory, but in reality those free meals aren't always filled with balanced nutrition, those free schools don't always offer the best education, and the service programs get cut and kids then have to fend for themselves. They can end up in prison or on the streets."

"Because they choose to."

"No, because they're forced to."

"Life always offers a choice."

"Some people need an environment where they feel safe. Look at this." Amera pulled out her tablet and showed him a video created by Peale House so that he could see some of the interior and exterior issues the money requested in the proposal would fix. The home consisted of a residential facility, where families and unattached individuals, including children, lived temporarily, until they found permanent housing. In the case of the children, either foster care or adoption. The remainder of the grounds was dedicated to providing services to newly arrived immigrants, especially those who had been granted asylum, where they were given training and skills to help them adjust to their new country. Peale House had become extremely popular with this population but was having a difficult time keeping up with the demand.

After watching two minutes of the video, he yawned then pointed to something. "Why isn't she dancing?"

"Who?" Amera asked surprised by the question. The scene showed her friend, Florence Dean, discussing the good Peale House did and showed her standing in the main living area of the residential facility that desperately needed repairs.

Curtis paused the video then pointed to a little girl of about seven, sitting in the corner making circles with her finger on the floor. "She's dressed in a tutu. Get her to dance next time and maybe I'll be interested."

Amera stopped the video and turned it off. "There's hardly any place for her to move. They don't have a designated play area and sometimes the kids play in the streets, which is very dangerous."

"Kids play in the streets all the time. The smart ones get out of the way when they see a car coming."

"It's still not--."

He sent her a hard look. "Have you gone deaf, Em?" he said using the nickname he'd given her years ago. "I said no." His shifted his gaze to the cars whizzing past on the freeway. "Don't put it on my desk again. I don't like their numbers."

"Their numbers?"

He tapped the back of his fingers against the window. "Are you a parrot now? Yes, the numbers."

Amera resisted the urge to smash her tablet against the back of his head. She shifted her gaze to the window. This was her baby and for the past three years she'd tried to get him to consider it. She knew the amount they were asking for was pocket change to him, but he didn't care. She glanced at the car trash bin filled with blood stained tissues. The color should be black instead of red, she thought. No, he wasn't human. He was cold and callous, just like his father. She hated when she forgot that, but she wouldn't next time.

"Do you know how many charities I donate to? If I funded everyone who asked, I'd have nothing left."

Amera glanced at him, surprised he even felt the need to defend himself. The charities he donated to weren't philanthropic decisions but business ones. The problem with Curtis was that he was smart. If he'd been charming, with no substance or ruthless without empathy, he wouldn't get under her skin. But there was something there. She hadn't been able to identify it yet. She wasn't sure if it was his brilliance, his dedication to maintain what his father and grandfather had built or just her dogged determination that kept her. She knew he hadn't made it to the top in his industry based on superficial flair or nepotism, the man was a wolverine with a brain of ferocious intellect.

He'd won the argument. He didn't have to convince her of anything. He was the boss. He was the one with the money and the power. She couldn't afford to forget that. He didn't have moments of weakness. His nosebleeds were just a nuisance, not a sign for compassion. She had to remember that also. She wondered why they always made her forget who he was. Especially because it was one of his nose bleeds that had gotten her the job in the first place.

"It's not going to be easy," the head of Human Resources, Miranda Layton, had told Amera, her voice trembling a little, as she led her to Curtis' office. Miranda was a brunette with tight lips who walked like a woman surrounded by a cloud of gnats. Her eyes darting from side to side in a distracted way, her hands moving with agitation to her neck and face at the oddest moments.

"I know," Amera said, as she had the previous ten times Miranda had warned her.

Ms. Layton vaguely pointed to a small room off to the side. "You'll work there," she said, then stopped in front of two large wooden doors, quickly tapped on one door then opened it as if she were afraid she'd lose courage and shoved Amera in front of her.

Curtis sat on his desk with his shirt partially open and his head held back, holding a tissue to his nose, another man stood over him undoing his shirt.

Miranda took a hasty step back, stumbling over her words. "I--I knocked but no one answered."

The man unbuttoning his shirt froze, the one with the tissue surged to his feet. "What the hell do you want?"

"Your new executive assistant is here."

"So what? Get out and close the door."

Miranda backed up, tugging on Amera's sleeve and said in a low, frightened voice, "Let's go."

Amera folded her arms, studying the scene with interest, as she stood in front of the door. "No, I'm ready to get to work." If it was going to be both her first and last day she was going to enjoy it. Miranda didn't argue. She sent Amera a nervous glance as if to say 'it's your funeral' before she hurried out, as if the cloud of gnats had turned into a swarm of bees.

"It's not what you think," the other man said.

"I'm Amera Thurston."

The man with the nosebleed turned his back to her and grabbed more tissues. "And I'm a man who really doesn't give a damn." He pressed the tissues to his nose and held his head back.

"I'm Owen DeWall," the other man said, stretching out his hand. He had silver and black hair and an apologetic smile. "You can probably guess who he is."

Amera nodded and quickly assessed the situation based on the blood she'd seen on Curtis' shirt and Owen's state of undress. "It won't work."

"What?" Owen asked.

"He got blood on his shirt and you're going to give him yours. But it won't work."

"Why not?"

She marched over to Curtis and pressed his head forward. "You're doing it wrong. If you want a nosebleed to stop, you hold your head forward and allow the blood to congeal. The other way can make you sick."

"Do I look like I feel the need for a lecture?" he said, but he kept his head down.

Owen held out his shirt. She shook her head. "I told you it won't work. Put it back on."

"It will work," Curtis said reaching for it.

She moved the shirt out of reach. "It won't fit. You're bigger than he is."

"We're about the same height."

"Except that he has the body of a runner and you have the body of a--." Her gaze swept over him as her mind searched frantically for the right words. Finding nothing suitable she said, "Your shoulders are too broad and your arms are long."

"I don't drag my knuckles along the ground, despite what you may have heard," he said.

"I'll come to my own conclusions," she said in a dry tone. "I haven't seen you walk yet."

Curtis' cell phone buzzed, interrupting his reply. He glanced down at a text and swore again. "He's in the building." They were located on the 24th floor and he knew he had only a few minutes before his father would come bursting into his office.

"Who?" Amera asked, wondering who could cause such strange behavior.

"Bishop Senior," Owen said.

His father was coming and that was a cause for concern. Amera noticed a closet off to the side and walked over and opened it. "And you don't have another shirt?"

"He did," Owen replied when Curtis didn't. "Until the last assistant tore them up with scissors and--."

"Do you think I'd be borrowing his, if I did?" Curtis cut in.

"You could order one and have someone stall him."

"You can't stall a Bishop and there's not enough time," Owen said. "Bishop Senior will be here in a minute."

"Just tell him what happened."

Owen shook his head. "He thinks the nosebleeds are a sign of weakness. Curtis will never live this down."

Curtis tossed the tissue away, his nosebleed had stopped, but his annoyance had only just begun. He shoved Amera towards the door. "Get out. We'll handle this."

"Put your shirt back on," Amera said, planting her feet firmly, making it difficult for him to budge her.

"What?"

"I know how to help you."

Curtis glanced at Owen who just shrugged.

"Do it," Amera said.

Curtis grabbed his soiled shirt and put it back on. "If this doesn't work, you're fired."

"I know. Come here," she said pointing to a spot near the wall. "Don't move."

Before he could ask why, Bishop Senior walked into the room. At the exact moment, Amera swung the closet door open wide and hit Curtis hard in the face. He stumbled back holding his nose.

"Oh, sir! I'm so sorry. Are you okay?" she said rushing over to him. She turned to Owen who stood stunned--his eyes wide and his mouth open. She pointed to the box of tissues. He blinked, coming out of his stupor then quickly handed them to her.

"Who the hell is this woman?" Bishop Senior demanded.

"The new executive assistant," Owen said.

"Is she usually this careless?" Bishop Senior said standing in the doorway. "Get another one."

"This is her first day."

"Sir, I'm so sorry," Amera said focusing on Curtis. "I

didn't see you." She grabbed a handful of tissues and held them out to him. He seized them and his eyes met hers-- dark brown eyes shining with pain, surprise and, respect.

She'd been by his side ever since. But that moment of connection had been rare. Amera looked at him now. He was still doing his father's dirty work and she was still cleaning up his nosebleeds.

"Where to now?" he said.

"The office. You have nothing else planned for today."

Back at headquarters Amera thought of how she was going to tell the people at Peale House that they'd have to look for another way to find the funding they needed to keep going, and the sad news the workers at the factory would be telling their families. She walked over to her desk, ready to sink into her chair then paused when she spotted the pink slip.

CHAPTER 2

Amera had expected a lot of things. But she hadn't expected a pink slip. She'd been hoping for a raise. When Curtis had made the announcement earlier at the factory, she hadn't imagined her job was also on the line. The loss of her job wouldn't just affect her, but she'd sent some money to Peale House and had hoped to secretly send Bill some money to help him care for his sons' needs while he looked for another job. Now she wouldn't have that option. She hadn't even gotten a warning. It would have been better if he'd told her in person. But that wasn't his way. She found his action cowardly, which wasn't like him. He'd been able to tell hundreds of workers they'd no longer have a job. Firing her shouldn't have been a problem. He'd fired many assistants before, but maybe it was better this way. If he told her face-to-face, she'd probably say things she'd later regret.

Amera immediately started to pack her things with a

cool rage. She thought of rebelling and fighting to remain, but she didn't want to be escorted out of the building by the security guards. At that moment, she wished she'd hit him with her fist instead of the door during their first meeting. But he had a thick head, she probably would have hurt her hand and he wasn't worth it.

Curtis walked by her office then backed up and stared at her for a long moment. "What the hell are you doing?"

She held up the pink slip.

He marched over to her and she saw a rare expression cross his face--a look of surprise. For a brief moment she saw how good looking he was. His looks had never really registered before. People rarely notice the majestic beauty of a lion when its teeth are stained with the blood of its prey. Like Curtis. He was too vicious to be considered attractive. She put another object in her box.

"You have two weeks," he said in a gruff tone.

She glanced up. "What?"

He tucked the note in his jacket pocket. "You have time. There's no need to pack up now."

"But--."

"Good. I'll see you tomorrow." He turned and left.

She started to follow him then stopped. She wouldn't quit right now. She'd put in her two weeks and get her check. That's when she decided she'd give him two weeks he'd never forget.

Curtis stared at the head of HR wondering if he'd misheard her. He leaned forward in his chair annoyed by her distracting habit of blinking at him and twitching. "What?"

Miranda cleared her throat in a nervous gesture and clasped then unclasped her hands. "I said she has to go."

"Why? What are the circumstances?"

"I was given orders."

"By whom?" he asked, but as he said the words he already knew the answer.

"Your father, I mean Bishop Senior said so."

Curtis bit the inside of his cheek so hard he tasted blood. He had to keep calm. Control was everything. He couldn't get angry, he couldn't get upset. Facts were neutral, how he responded to them was all that mattered. 'Never let them know how you feel,' his father had taught him. *The damn bastard.* Why couldn't he have told him what he was up to instead of making him look like a fool? Why couldn't he start treating him like an equal instead of a minion? But then his father didn't have an equal. He was the ruler--the man who must be obeyed.

Miranda plastered on a smile that made her look sick instead of happy. "I'm sure Ms. Thurston will get a great-_"

Curtis held up his hand, silencing her. He didn't like her false cheery tone. He knew she was caught in the middle of a power play that made her feel uncomfortable, but he didn't care. He had to figure out his next strategy. He pulled the pink slip from his pocket and placed it on the desk. He kept his gaze lowered and slid it across the desk. "This didn't happen."

"But--"

"For now," he added, slowly lifting his gaze to meet hers. "Understood?"

Miranda swallowed and nodded, even though from her expression she clearly didn't understand what he was talking about.

Curtis tapped the desk with his knuckles. "Good," he said standing. He left the HR department and returned to his office as though nothing had happened. He shut the door with a soft click, stood in front of his large window, then stared down at the sight of his biggest failure--a venture his father would never let him forget. Several years ago, he'd spent an enormous amount of money and resources on a new innovative drive-through drug store. It had bombed. The building could have been bulldozed or cleared, but his father wouldn't let anyone touch it. And every day when Curtis looked out his window he was reminded of how far he'd fallen short of his father's greatness. It didn't matter that he'd recently saved the parent company millions. Over the last year he'd shown how good he was. He'd raised profits by fifty percent and partnered with three big companies and licensed rights to other companies to use several devices they had patented. But he was still not as good as the great and mighty Benjamin Bishop.

His father still wanted to keep him in line. Wanted to remind him who was boss. His father's current action, to fire Amera, was a chess move and Curtis decided he would make one of his own. Winners and losers, that's all life was about. He'd received that lesson early as a young boy. He remembered going to Thailand to visit one of their factories with his grandfather, who'd Anglicized their family name to Bishop when he'd come to America, and created a booming worldwide business in clothing manufacturing.

Curtis remembered driving through the streets of Thailand, in their plush car wanting to go back to play with the baby elephant at the hotel and talk to its trainer. But his grandfather had told him he had to see what he would inherit one day, and by then he'd already learned the responsibility he had to carry. On that particular day, before they reached the garment factory, Curtis saw people running, some screaming and many fighting. He saw large wooden signs lying on the ground and people too, lots of them--some with blood seeping from wounds. He saw people hitting others with baseball bats and the sight scared him. "What's going on?"

"We're taking care of the cockroaches," his grandfather had said. "The ingrates that try to feed off us." Curtis later learned that his grandfather had taken care of the picketing workers and Curtis had never asked why they were unhappy, having learned early that his grandfather liked to clamp down any signs of a soft heart. At times, using his cane against Curtis' shins to make his message clear.

When he was older, his father had taken him on a helicopter flight over New York City, and had him look down at the bustling cars and crowds of people. "See how small people are from up here? That's how you have to see them--always. Like rodents, otherwise they'll destroy you like the Black Plague."

Curtis shoved his hands in his pocket, then rested his forehead against the cool glass of the window. He didn't see people as cockroaches or rodents. He tried his best not to see them at all. They were a necessary evil, tools for winners. He didn't know why his father had made such an unexpected move with Amera, but he'd find out and make him understand that he didn't plan to stand in his shadow forever.

Someone knocked on the door.

"What?" he snapped, keeping his gaze on the empty building outside.

"How many holidays have you ruined this year?" his half brother, Kyle Carroll, said closing the door behind him. There was a seven year age gap between the two and they looked nothing alike, although they shared the same mother. Kyle always had a grin and kind word for others.

Curtis didn't turn around. He hated his brother's annual visits. "What do you want?"

He heard his brother pick up something and skim through it. " Peale House? Sounds interesting. Looks like another proposal from Ms. Thurston."

"You can take it and use it as a sleep aid."

Kyle tossed the brochure down. "Stop being such a jerk. I'm sure they made a good effort and worked hard on it."

"More's the pity."

"If I had the money--"

Curtis slowly turned and looked directly at his brother. "Right, but you don't."

Kyle shrugged. "I get by and I'm happy."

Curtis lifted a brow and flashed a malicious grin. "Really?"

For a second, his brother's carefree veneer slipped. "Yes."

"Good." Curtis sat behind his desk and steepled his fingers. "Let's not pretend you've come here looking for brotherly love. The only reason you stomach me is because I'm worth it. What do you want?"

"Mom wants to know if you'll be coming for Christmas."

Curtis drummed his fingers against each other. "Remind me. What did I say last year?"

Kyle fell into a chair and sighed. "No."

"And what do you think I'll say next year?"

"Come on. It's once a year and it would be nice to have you."

"Really? How long did you have to practice saying that without throwing up?"

Kyle folded his arms. "I mean it."

Curtis glanced at the ring on his brother's finger. "Still married?"

"Yes. We're expecting our second child."

Curtis looked at his brother for a long moment, sensing something not right. "You don't sound happy. Was it an unexpected surprise?"

"Of course I'm happy."

Curtis nodded. "That's right," he said with a note of sarcasm. "Congratulations. You and your little family, and Mom, can be happy and celebrate without me."

Kyle shook his head. "You know, one day Mom may stop asking you and I'll stop coming."

"Why wait? You can start now."

"You don't have to keep acting like a bastard just to please him."

"I'm not acting." Curtis held his brother's gaze. "Don't try to make me out to be someone I'm not." He leaned back in his chair and glanced at his watch. "Do you want anything else?"

"Yes, to know why Mom even cares about you anymore."

"You should ask her. And when you do, tell her to stop." He stood and grabbed his jacket. "We're done?"

"I'd say we're finished."

"Good." Curtis nodded then left.

Kyle stood up and kicked his chair, toppling it over. Damn, he wished he didn't let his brother get to him. He righted the chair just as Amera entered the room carrying a manila folder. "You're still here?" he asked watching her set the folder on his brother's desk. "I don't know how you've managed to last this long."

"It's a job."

"You could get other jobs."

"It's a challenge."

"So is being a lion tamer, but not many people sign up for a job like that."

"Forget about him."

"I can't. I wish I could, but every holiday his absence at our annual family gathering seems to grow and my mother misses him more and more. I hate seeing her so unhappy."

Amera leaned against the desk and folded her arms. It wasn't an aggressive move, but somehow it felt like a powerful one, as if she were taking charge of the situation. "She'll remain that way until she stops wishing things were different."

"You're telling me not to come back."

"I don't believe that's what I said."

He couldn't read her and he could read most women. Women liked his good looks and charm, but while he didn't sense Amera didn't like him, he didn't get the sense she liked him either. She had a hard edge that unsettled him. "So what do you expect me to do?"

"I don't expect you to do anything. It's up to you whether you'll accept that he's not going to change. Wanting things to be different than they are will only hurt you, *and* your mother."

"You know from experience?"

Amera blinked slowly, then pushed herself from the desk. "It's a lesson few people wish to learn."

He wasn't surprised by her vague response. She remained a mystery to him. "Happy holidays. Think he'd noticed if I left a lump of coal on his desk?"

"He'd just find a use for it."

Curtis rested his hands at the foot of his father's massive, sleigh oak bed ready to do battle. His father had aged and his illness had given his face a cadaverous look, but he still maintained the menacing air of a raptor.

"My executive assistant stays," Curtis said, maintaining an even, almost, cordial tone. He'd learned early that riling his father was never a good counter-strategy.

Bishop Senior took off his oxygen mask and pinned his son with a dark look, a cold smile touching the corners of his mouth. "She doesn't if I say so."

"She's not going anywhere."

"Why? You don't need her. You're using her as an excuse."

"An excuse for what?"

"To not get married. You don't need an assistant. Get yourself a wife. It's about time and it will save the company money."

Curtis tapped his chest. "I am in control of who does or doesn't works for me."

"It's my business and this recent hire--"

"She isn't recent."

His father's gaze sharpened. "How long has she been with you?"

"Long enough to know my ways. I don't want to train anyone else."

"How long?"

Curtis gritted his teeth. "Long enough to--"

"How long?" he snapped.

"Five years."

Bishop Senior swore and shook his head. "My God. I wasn't even married to your mother that long."

"She's an excellent worker--"

"And she's made you soft," his father finished with a note of disgust. "When I was your age and running this business, profits were through the roof."

"I've doubled them."

"Why not triple them? Quadruple them? And what new markets have you dominated? Which of our competitors have you destroyed? None."

"Times have changed. I don't think you need to destroy--"

"Come here."

Curtis gripped his hands into fists. "Father."

"I said come here," he repeated in a hard tone, which commanded obedience.

Curtis sighed then walked to his father's side.

Bishop Senior grabbed the front of his son's shirt, pulled him down with surprising strength and slapped him hard across the face. "Do I need to remind you about the rise of Western dominance?" he said yanking Curtis' face close to his and slapping him again. "How in the fifteenth century India and China ruled the markets until the Europeans accidentally discovered the riches of America and improved their maritime power?"

"Father," Curtis said in a whisper.

He slapped him once more. "How industrialization helped them to destroy other nations? How the Dutch, the Portuguese, the Spanish talked about carving up the

African continent and did so with brutal mastery?" He tightened his grip, his eyes blazing with rage. "Dominance is always about destruction. Don't you ever forget that." He shoved his son away.

Curtis stumbled back, but quickly regained his footing, being careful not to touch his stinging face.

"Come here."

Curtis steeled himself and again, moved in close.

Bishop Senior reached out and straightened his son's tie then smoothed it down. To an outsider it looked like an affectionate gesture, but both men knew it wasn't. "Did you talk to the people at Valdan?"

"Yes."

"I should never have listened to you and brought one of our factories to a town with a whole bunch of whiny babies. We could have made a lot more abroad with a cheaper labor force and higher quality. But you thought this town was perfect."

"We got the building cheap and it's making us money."

"Not enough, and they've gotten soft. I heard you're giving them bonuses. Why? You trying to be their friend? They don't care. People like to have someone to fear." He pointed at him. "That's your biggest problem. You'll never be as good as me. Until you fully understand that...." He took several moments to catch his breath. "You're just pathetic. Cut the costs on the holiday party and the bonuses."

Curtis bit his cheek and silently counted to ten. Even though he never attended the holiday party, he knew that was one event many of the employees at headquarters looked forward to. "It helps morale." Curtis knew that news of Valdan closing at the end of the month would affect people at headquarters and he wanted to show them that business was still good.

"I don't care."

"We've got a good team."

"And you're afraid of losing them?" He shook his head. "Rats will feed on whatever you give them. Let them quit, if they want to. If you worry about them, then they own you. If you care, they can manipulate you. Do I have to remind you of this every year? I don't care what they do. People can quit. But where will they go in this economy? With what we're paying? I'd like to see them try. You're job is to do what *I* say. You're just my puppet, don't start getting strange ideas that you matter around here. No one would miss you. *I'll* be missed. My blood is on every item, every brick. Bishop Enterprises bears my name. You're only standing there because of me. I gave you life and I gave you a purpose. You owe me."

"It costs more money to retrain key people. In the long run, the party keeps our profits high by reminding people who to be loyal to."

Bishop Senior narrowed his eyes. "Are you saying you're determined to give the rats their little piece of cheese?"

"Yes."

He shrugged. "Fine. You win this round. Have you spoken to your mother?"

Curtis hesitated, startled by the change of topic. "No."

"Do you plan to?"

"No."

"Her son is married with a kid. You know I don't like to be outdone. You're getting rid of your assistant and getting a wife. I want an heir. Make it happen."

He wasn't getting rid of Amera, Curtis silently vowed as he left his father's bedroom and walked down the stairs of the elaborate mansion he'd grown up in. If his father wanted him to have a wife, he'd get one, but his work life was his. He shoved his hands in his pockets, not fully understanding why his father's demand made him so angry. It shouldn't. He'd gotten rid of assistants before. But *he'd* done the firing. The sight of the pink slip in Amera's hand infuriated him. It made the action feel personal. He should have told him first. It was the principle of the thing. But that conclusion still didn't satisfy him. There was something else that bothered him, he just didn't know what.

Curtis silently swore, passing by the household staff who went out of their way to shift their gaze away from him when he walked past. Only his footsteps could be heard on the marble tile, they'd learned to move about like ghosts, being as unobtrusive as possible. He didn't know their names or faces and didn't care to. The dark paneled walls had the same solemn sheen of a house that absorbed sunlight, casting everything in shadow, no matter how bright the day. Curtis walked out the front door, briefly shielding his eyes against the sun. The cold, crisp day swept a blanket of blue across the sky. It probably wouldn't snow until the New Year.

"Where to?" his driver asked, holding the door open.

Curtis got into the backseat, for a moment wishing he had Em to plan his schedule. Had he become too dependent on her? He touched his sore jaw. Maybe it was good for his father to slap some sense into him. He had to remain focused. It was time for him to marry and start a family to continue the bloodline.

"Sir?"

He glanced up at the driver annoyed. "What?"

"Where to?"

He sighed and let his hand fall. "Just drive, I don't care," he said feeling lost.

Amera sat at her desk and drummed her fingers, trying to formulate the best way to get back at Curtis. Closing the factory was bad enough, then dismissing her proposal, but nothing had prepared her for being fired – not after all her dedication over the past five years. Fortunately, two weeks was plenty of time to come up with a plan. She wouldn't let him get rid of her so easily, without at least feeling the sting of her wrath.

She looked at her watch and increased her drumming. She hadn't heard from him in nearly two hours.

That was rare. He always had her doing something. He'd blindsided her twice, first with the factory and then the pink slip, was he preparing for another blow? Or could something be wrong? No, he was probably trying to show her how much she'd already lost her usefulness. Maybe he really wanted to make her angry enough so that she would quit before the end of two weeks. She flattened her hand on the desk. He'd be disappointed. But then again, maybe she'd accepted his bad behavior for too long. Maybe she should just pack her things and disappear. She was about to reach for her box when her phone rang.

"I need to buy a ring," Curtis said, without preamble. "Make an appointment."

"A ring?" Amera repeated just to make sure. She'd never seen him wear jewelry before.

"Yes, an engagement ring. I want the jeweler in my office by tomorrow."

"An engagement ring?"

"Yes, my little parrot. Isn't that what I just said?"

A ring? He was going to get married? Really? She shook her head. That was none of her business, even though most of his life had been. She knew a lot about him, although he didn't have much of a life outside of work. She guessed it was instructions from 'on high'. He was at the right age and the old man would want to see him settled before he died. Curtis hadn't shown any interest in any particular woman, but had casually being seeing Crystal Montrose the daughter of a prominent senator. She seemed the best likely candidate.

"Tomorrow is too soon," Amera said, automatically

thinking over all the details and tasks she would need to get done in order for his proposal of marriage to work. He was not a romantic and if he wanted to have a fiancée by the end of the week, Amera knew she would have to make sure everything was flawless.

"Why?"

"Do you want her to say yes?"

"That's the plan," he said in a dry tone.

"Then give me two days and I'll prepare everything."

"Two days?"

"Yes, my little parrot," she said in a cool tone. "Isn't that what I just said?"

Silence greeted her from the other end, but she knew he didn't mind when she threw his words back at him. Besides, in two weeks she'd be gone anyway. She switched the phone to her other ear and waited for him to argue.

"Good," he said then hung up.

Amera set her phone down and leaned back in her chair. Bishop wanted a bride. She already felt sorry for the woman, but at least it would keep her busy. Keeping busy had always been the best way for her to get through the holidays since it was usually a lonely experience for her.

Amera dove into her assigned task with ruthless efficiency, briefly forgetting about her plan for revenge. She contacted an established florist, a renowned chef and local jeweler, and made a reservation at an exclusive hotel. The following day, she took off some time and went to a local specialty store looking to find something extra special for the occasion. That's when she spotted an angel figurine sitting in one of the displays. She knew Crystal loved angels. It would add a nice touch.

"How much is that?" she asked the clerk, a middle aged man with jowls that reminded her of a bloodhound.

The clerk looked up and sent her a bored look. "Sorry, it's not for sale."

"I'll pay--"

"I said it's not for sale. Sorry, those are the boss's orders."

She wished he'd stop saying he was 'sorry', when he clearly didn't mean it. Amera looked around for something else when an attractive black woman, who smelled of expensive perfume and looked as if she'd just stepped off of a runaway, brushed past her and gazed at the angel. "Oh that's beautiful. I could just see it on my mantle. How much is it?"

"It's not for--" He started to say, before he looked up and his bored tone and expression vanished.

"Are you sure I couldn't talk to someone?" the woman said displaying a flirtatious grin.

The clerk leaned against the counter, as if he were a gambler ready to get a hot tip. "How much are you willing to offer?"

The woman looked up at the ceiling and tapped her chin then said, "A hundred."

"That sounds like the right price to me. It's yours."

Amera walked up to them. "I thought you said it wasn't for sale."

The man turned his back and opened up the curio. "You didn't give me a price."

Amera looked at the other woman without malice. Clearly the price of entry was a gorgeous face and a great body. She knew that getting Crystal to say yes to Curtis' proposal would take a little more persuasion and this angel could be the ticket. "Three hundred," she said.

"Sorry," the clerk said, again giving the word little meaning. He reached down and took out several sheets of white tissue paper from beneath the counter and began to wrap the figurine. "I already accepted her offer ."

"Of course," Amera said acknowledging defeat. She turned.

The woman grabbed Amera's coat sleeve before she could leave. "Wait. Do you really want it?"

"It doesn't matter," Amera said, embarrassed by the woman's look of pity.

"I don't want to take what isn't mine."

Amera looked at the woman's fashionable, high-end clothes and exquisite face. The clerk couldn't help it. He'd wanted to impress her. Most men would. "It was yours the moment you walked in. Excuse me." She left, but in her haste forgot the step that led up to the door and tumbled forward, falling flat on her face. She quickly jumped to her feet, hoping nobody noticed and wiped her coat.

"Are you okay?" the woman asked rushing up to her, with the sales clerk close behind.

"I'm fine."

"But your--"

"I'm really busy. Excuse me," she said and hurried past her, feeling a mixture of anger and humiliation.

The next day Amera arrived at the hotel, an hour earlier, to organize the lavish suite, removing the one wilted bloom she saw in one of the four bouquets she had ordered--Curtis would have noticed. She dimmed the lights and arranged the candles, keenly aware of the touches of the season that decorated the room. A warm fire blazed, casting an amber glow throughout the main sitting area, accentuating the light scent of cinnamon. The room was set for a romantic holiday engagement, and the exact replica of a scene she'd read in a book.

She didn't like Curtis--nobody did--but for a moment she envied Crystal. She wished that one day someone would treat her like a princess. Like she mattered to them, and she didn't care if he hired someone else, like Curtis had, to make that impression. One day she wanted to dress up in elegant clothes and go out on the town and dine at the finest restaurants and live a life of glamour.

But Amera knew she'd have no romance this holiday season. There would be no gathering of family and friends. She had a couple of friends, but never wanted to be a bother and she didn't have any family. It would be the same as last year and the year before that. She'd pretend that Christmas was just another ordinary day. She'd lock herself away, do a reading marathon and then start the New Year. Amera pulled herself out of her slight melancholy and snapped back into the present. Although she'd never experience such a moment, she would make the evening perfect for Crystal and live vicariously.

"It's too dark," Curtis said coming into the room. He turned up the lights.

Amera turned them back down. "I'm trying to create the perfect mood."

He turned them up again. "I like to see what I'm doing." Before she could respond he grabbed her chin and turned her head. "What the hell happened to your face?"

She jerked her head back, startled. "My face?"

"Haven't you looked in a mirror?"

"I've been too busy working," Amera said going to the bathroom, knowing she'd get no faint praise from him. She looked at her reflection in the mirror and gasped. She had a large bruise under her eye. She hadn't seen it this morning because she'd been so busy. At least it explained why the hotel and wait staff had been looking at her strangely.

"So what did you do?" Curtis asked from behind her.

She spun around and saw him standing in the doorway, still in his overcoat, looking about as cuddly as a cactus. She did not want to tell him that she'd fallen on her face. She walked over to him and reached for his coat. "She'll be here in a moment. You should get comfortable."

"You haven't answered my question."

Amera draped his coat over her arm. "It's not like you to care, sir," she said, then made a move to walk past him.

He blocked her, making excellent use of his broad chest and height, but kept his voice low. "And it's not like you to not answer me, Em."

She raised her gaze and calmly held his intense dark eyes. "I don't want to."

"You have to."

She lifted one of his hands and stared down at his knuckles. "It's amazing how you've managed to walk upright for so long."

Someone knocked on the door interrupting his reply. "That's probably her. Now go sit down," she ordered then opened the door. It was the jeweler. She ushered him in and gave him a few brief instructions before leading him to a small room. She hung up Curtis' coat and again, adjusted the lighting.

She felt ashamed that she'd briefly wanted to trade places with Crystal. Organizing details and being in the background was what her life was about and what it would always be. She'd fallen short of her own rules. Rules she'd learned as a refugee. Don't stand out. Don't want what you can't have. Don't strive for mediocrity. Never fail. She didn't stand out, she made sure of that, always wearing a handful of selected items to work, which she called her uniform. She was grateful for her job and her salary, which afforded her a comfortable living, but she had failed in getting funding for Peale House and taking care of Bill and his family and with each year she seemed to grow more restless. She couldn't understand why. Since immigrating to America, she'd never had a cold hungry night, like what she had experienced when she was on her own in the refugee camp. Alone and afraid.

She turned to look at Curtis who stubbornly refused to sit, but instead stood by the window, his hands clasped behind his back, looking down at the street traffic. He was the embodiment of power and wealth, but strangely she didn't envy him. The image made her sad because all she saw was stark loneliness that made her heart twist. She turned away disgusted with herself. She couldn't afford to feel sorry for him. He didn't deserve it. He liked his life exactly the way he designed it and soon--he'd have a fiancée and she'd never see him again. The jeweler sat quietly in the small room off to the side of the suite, looking out of place. He had wanted to show Curtis the collection of rings he had selected, but Curtis had brusquely said that he'd wait for his bride to arrive, before making a selection.

Amera pressed her hands together and did a final look around the room. Crystal will love this, she thought.

Unfortunately, Crystal didn't show up.

$\mathcal{A}$mera sat in a far corner of the suite waiting to hear from the front desk, but the call never came. After an hour, she sent Curtis a glance. He looked bored, but not angry. Twice she'd had to calm the chef who had prepared a menu consisting of an assortment of dishes that needed to be served within a certain time-frame. Her perfect proposal was going all wrong. Would Curtis think she did something wrong, like give Crystal the wrong address or time? She had been clear. Had Crystal been delayed? She was usually always on time. Amera took out her cell phone to call. It rang just as she started to dial. She breathed a sigh of relief when she recognized the number. She jumped up, said, "Excuse me," then went into the bedroom suite and closed the door.

"Where are you?" she asked.

"Is he still there?"

"Of course," Amera said surprised by the question. "He's waiting for you."

"Is he angry?"

"Where are you? Is something wrong?"

"I'm nervous."

"Why?"

"He's never done something like this before. He's going to ask me to marry him, isn't he?"

Amera hesitated, wondering if she should spoil the surprise. "Come by and find out."

"Oh my god he is," Crystal said with a note of terror.

"If you'll just come and--"

"He shouldn't," she interrupted, sounding miserable. "He's only doing it because that's what our families want. Mainly, what his father wants."

"I'm sure he wants it too. He takes commitment seriously and you should see--"

"I'm sure you did it all," she said and Amera could hear the smile in her voice. "You're the best. I know that all the restaurants, shows and gifts were because of you."

"I just help," Amera said embarrassed by Crystal's praise. She was just an assistant doing the job she was paid to do. "I don't--"

"He should marry you. You're able to deal with him better than anyone. You've been with him long enough. Longer than most. He scares me."

"I know marriage is a big decision, but just come over and have dinner with him--."

"I was only with him because I was frightened not to

be, but I can't do it anymore. He's heartless. Tell him I don't want to see him again."

"You tell him."

"I know I'm a coward and I'm sorry to put you in this position, but I can't face him. I'll make it up to you."

"Crystal you're just--" Amera paused when she heard a click. "Crystal? Crystal?" Amera silently swore, then called her back, but the phone kept ringing. What should she do? She hadn't planned for this. She'd at least hoped Crystal would have shown up. Not only hadn't she shown up but she'd talked nonsense. At one moment calling Curtis 'heartless' then suggesting Amera marry him! Was she saying that Amera was cold too? Amera shook her head. She couldn't worry about that now. She stared at the bedroom door. It was the only thing that separated her from an awful task. She rehearsed in her mind different ways to break the news. She could lie and say something unexpected had come up. Or she could question his judgment about Crystal's suitability. But he'd see through both. Being direct was the best option. She would tell him quickly and then go home. He'd just nod his head in a stoic manner and then dismiss her. She took a deep breath then returned to the main lounge. Curtis had returned to his post at the window and had his back to her. "Sir--"

"Did you bump into a door or something?"

Amera blinked. "What?"

"I'm still curious about that bruise. Come here."

She knew he was just toying with her and she wasn't

in the mood for his strange games. She stayed put and folded her arms. "I just spoke to Crystal."

"It's snowing. I didn't think it would."

"And Crystal said--"

"Come and see it."

"Sir, I'm trying to tell you--"

"I thought you liked snow. Come here."

Amera threw up her hands in exasperation. The man was insufferable. He never cared about her feelings before and she couldn't understand his strange calm. She made a crude gesture, behind his back and mimed strangling him with her hands and wringing his neck then joined him at the window. She saw the tiny white lights on the trees surrounding the hotel and the car beams piercing the black night, but she didn't see any snow. It was barely past five o'clock but looked like midnight. "I don't see anything."

He pointed to a lamppost. "You can see it falling there."

He was right. Under the yellow glow of the lamppost, she could see the soft white powder falling. She couldn't understand his interest, considering the woman he'd hoped to marry hadn't shown up yet. "It won't stay."

He nodded. "You're right." He tapped the glass. "Do you know what's good about this window?"

"What?" Amera asked with little interest.

He looked at her, a faint glint of humor in his eyes. "I can see what's going on behind me."

She stiffened, her cheeks burning, remembering the gestures she'd made behind his back. She lowered her gaze. "I'm sorry, sir. It was a moment of frustration, especially since..." she let her words die away.

"Since what?"

Since you've dropped me after five years of excellent service, giving me only two weeks' notice without the decency of telling me why I'm being let go. Even though you know I'm the best and I deserve better. But Amera wisely kept those thoughts to herself. She took a deep breath and raised her eyes to his dark gaze. A look that had never intimidated her. "Since I'll be gone soon."

His eyes became as flat and unreadable as granite. "Right," he said, then shifted his gaze back to the window.

"Sir, about Crystal."

Curtis turned to her then said in a bored tone. "She's not coming." He motioned to the waiter and walked over to the dining table. "Let's eat."

The waiter eagerly dashed off to let the chef know they were ready.

"But--."

He sat down. "But what? I'm hungry."

Amera sat in the chair in front of him, not sure he understood the severity of the situation. "Sir--"

He held up his hand. "Wait until the third course."

Amera sighed and they ate the first two courses in silence. When she was finished she said, "Crystal doesn't want to see you again."

"That's a relief," he said, just as the waiter set down the third course, one of Crystal's favorites: roasted leg of lamb, garnished with slices of stewed guava jelly, a sweet tropical fruit, served on a bed of white rice, French beans with sliced almonds, and a side order of freshly baked rolls, and, of course, champagne.

"A relief?"

He lifted his utensils and shook his head. "Come on my little parrot. Don't tell me you're really surprised."

"I at least expected her to show up. It's not my place to know the inner workings of your personal life, but this is odd even for you."

"Even for me?"

"The woman you'd hoped to marry says she never wants to see you again and you're eating dinner as if nothing has happened."

"I figured as much."

"And you don't care?" Amera shook her head, realizing how ridiculous her words were. "I'm sorry, of course you don't."

"And if I did care, is that going to change her mind?" He shrugged. "Disappointment is a part of life." He pointed at her plate. "Your food is getting cold."

Amera glanced down at her plate and calculated the six course meal in despair. She'd ordered too much, but Crystal always liked to have a choice. "We can't finish all this."

"Let me guess," Curtis said spearing a bean. "You want to donate the leftovers somewhere."

"It's a thought."

"Will you regain your appetite if I say yes?"

She nodded.

"Fine. Tell them to bag the rest and send it to whatever address you want."

"Thank you, sir," she said then began to eat. She'd never eaten alone with him before. And in such an intimate setting, she felt stiff and awkward. He was a jerk, but his table manners were impeccable, something she'd taken years to learn. She remembered that at the second orphanage where she had lived, which had been established by a strict English socialite, education, 'social' manners and graces were emphasized. Knowing which fork or spoon to use, and when, was paramount to good manners, and Amera had been one of her favorite students.

"A bird?" he said when the fourth course came.

"I'm sorry?"

"That's how you got the bruise."

"Why do you keep coming back to that?"

"Because I find it amusing that my perfect Em has a few failings."

"I got caught in a hold up and the criminal exchanged gunfire with the police and I got cut by the shattering glass."

He looked at her for a long moment then shook his head and returned his gaze to his meal. "No, I bet you just tripped and fell."

She rested her napkin on the table and stood. "I'll go now."

"Not yet."

"You need something else?"

"I want you to choose a ring."

Amera fell back into her seat. Maybe he hadn't understood her before. "Crystal isn't coming. She--she doesn't want to see you again."

"I know that."

"Then why do you want to give her a ring?"

"The ring is for you."

Amera placed a hand on her chest, her heart picking up pace in growing anger. "Are you trying to mock me?"

"No, I just find it amusing that we somehow ended up with matching scars."

"What?"

He tapped the side of his cheek. "I tripped too, figuratively speaking."

Amera stared at him. She didn't understand what he was talking about. She turned up the lights and looked at him again, this time seeing the tiny scar on the side of his face. She hadn't noticed it before and he'd cleverly covered most of it with some makeup, but there was a slight swelling that gave it away.

"Well it was bound to happen," Amera said with an air of nonchalance.

"What?"

"One of the workers punching you."

To her surprise the corner of his mouth kicked up in a quick grin and he nodded. "Now choose a ring." Curtis called to the jeweler to join them. "He came all this way, let's make it worth his while." He lifted a glass of wine. "Don't worry, I won't ask you to marry me." A malicious grin crossed his face. "Though that would annoy the old man, wouldn't it? I could just imagine his face if I showed up with you as my fiancée."

"That's something you'd only have the pleasure of imagining because I'd never marry you."

Curtis sipped his wine, unfazed by her words then set the glass down. "Go on. I said choose one."

"But--"

"I thought women liked large sparkly things. Especially when they're expensive."

"Sir."

Curtis picked one up. "I think this one looks nice. No, wait," he said putting it down and picking up another. "This one is better." He shoved it on her ring finger then held up her hand. "Mrs. Curtis Bishop," he said to himself in a low, grim tone.

Amera pulled her hand away, a shadow of unease coursing through her. "Sir?"

"Okay," he said with a dismissive wave of his hand. "You're free to go now."

"But, sir--"

"Good night, Em."

Amera bit back a sigh of frustration. "Good night," she said, getting her coat. She briefly wondered who'd he'd select as Crystal's replacement, but then cast the thought aside. She wouldn't be around to find out.

CHAPTER 4

"*I* told you not to try. The man has a heart made of ice."

"Hmm," Amera said, hanging up her thick winter coat in the tiny office her friend Florence Dean used at Peale House. After the ruined proposal dinner, and Curtis' cryptic behavior, Amera didn't feel like going home just yet and decided to visit her friend. Meeting her had been fortuitous. She'd met the attractive brown skinned woman with elaborately designed tight braids and a big smile at a holding facility, when she had first arrived in the US, and then lost touch. They had only been there for two days, before they were separated, and sent to different parts of the country.

Florence's upbringing had been harder than hers. Amera had the benefit of a good education. Amera had no memory of living anywhere but in an orphanage, and being told stories of how she was left on the doorsteps of the first orphanage at about three years old, with a note:

"This is my daughter, America, please take care of her."
She was called Amera for short, and given the surname
Thurston, when she was christened by the people who
ran the orphanage, an independent Christian organization. She later learned she was one of five children to be
dropped off that day. Her memory of the orphanage
didn't stand out, but she didn't have any terrifying tales
either. Amera lived there until she was about seven, then
it closed and all the children were transferred to
Wenthrop Children's Home, a privately run facility. This
was where she got a solid education. The founder of the
home believed in strict discipline, not cruel, and education was paramount. She stayed at the children's home
until she was eighteen, gaining experience working with
the younger children, as she took on the role of being a
big sister to most of them. Then the war came. Florence
wasn't so lucky. She had been raised in a small West
African village, and had been the only girl, amongst six
brothers.

Her mother was a sickly woman, so by the time
Florence was six, she was forced to do most of the chores,
and soon found herself taking care of the family. She was
unable to go to school on a regular basis, but had been
able to get some schooling, on and off, until she was
forced to drop out when she turned thirteen. That's
when she was promised in marriage to a man three times
her age, and decided to run off to the main town to make
a better life for herself. Unfortunately, she found things
more difficult, and eventually ended up using her body to
survive on the streets, before she was taken in by a Chris-

tian Humanitarian AID organization, where she eventually finished her high school education, and got an opportunity to go to America.

After losing touch, Amera had come across Peale House quite by accident, after seeing the artwork of one of the residents featured in a local newspaper and then spotting Florence's face. Amera contacted her right away and they had had a heartfelt reunion, taking care to only talk about the present instead of the pain from the past. Amera was eager to help her friend with her efforts, wanting to give back the advantages she'd had at the orphanage and Wenthrop Children's Home. She knew the importance and power of education and hard work. So for the past three years she'd tried to get the additional funding Peale House needed to expand and provide better services for their clients.

But she had become frustrated. Over the past three years, she had helped them try several approaches to get funding from Curtis' company and others like his. Trying to gain interest through different means such as a newsletter, writing articles, having an on-line blog, and even creating several videos featuring the services they offered. But each year the answer was the same—no--and interest in the facility remained negligible. She couldn't gain the extra funding they needed, which didn't make sense to her. She was used to succeeding.

On several occasions, Florence tried to persuade her to stop. She told her that Peale House was getting by and doing what it was committed to, in spite of the lack of funding, but Amera wouldn't give up. She wasn't used to failing and wouldn't start now.

"Thanks for the food you sent. It really made the volunteers happy."

"I caught him during a moment of weakness. Not that he has many," Amera said thinking of Curtis' refusal to fund the proposal. She took off her gloves and sat down.

Her friend stared at her. "Why didn't you tell me?"

Amera blinked confused. "Tell you what?"

"That you're getting married?" Florence said, her gaze fixated on Amera's hand.

Amera glanced down at the ring. She'd completely forgotten about it. "No, Curtis gave it to me. As a joke," she quickly added when Florence's eyes widened. "It's nothing serious."

Florence came around the desk and lifted Amera's hand. "It looks pretty serious to me."

"His marriage proposal, or rather non-proposal, went south and he wanted to spend money. It's nothing."

"No, don't take it off," Florence said covering Amera's hand before she could remove the ring. "It looks so good on you. You chose the right one."

"I didn't choose it, he did."

Florence clicked her tongue. "He's a bastard, but he's got great taste."

"If it weren't for the nosebleeds, I wouldn't even think he was human."

"The what?" Florence asked returning to her chair.

"Never mind," Amera quickly said, ashamed that she'd even mentioned them.

"How long is he going to be the only man in your life?"

"What?"

"Aren't you even interested in having a normal life and relationship? You've been working for him for five years!"

"I have a normal life and relationships are not on the agenda." She didn't want to tell her friend about being let go.

Florence pointed at her. "That's your problem, you should stop living by agendas."

Amera looked at the ring, thoughtful. "I wonder how much I could get for this?"

"Don't sell it."

"Why not? You could use the money."

"True, but I don't want it that way. Keep it at least until the New Year. It's a gift, you should accept it. It's the holiday season, remember?"

It's something I try to forget. "Hmmm." She stood. "Well, I just came by to tell you the status of things."

"I wish you wouldn't worry about us. We're managing."

"You should be thriving," Amera said putting on her coat. She felt her friend settled for too little. She left the office and headed down the hall when a flash of pink caught her eye. She stopped and looked inside the dining room and saw the same little girl from her video wearing a tutu, sitting in the corner.

"Shouldn't she be in bed?"

"Yes, she should. Maya!" Florence said and the little girl's head snapped up and her eyes widened with fear.

"Wait," Amera said before Florence could scold her. "I want to talk to her."

"She's being--"

"Just give me a second." Amera walked over to the little girl, Curtis' words echoing in her mind. *Why isn't she dancing? Get her to dance next time and maybe I'll be interested.* She didn't believe him, but it was worth a shot. "Would you dance for me?"

The little girl's eyes lit up with joy then her expression grew wary.

"You don't believe me?"

She shook her head.

Amera knelt down to her level. "My name is Ms. Thurston and I work with a nasty old grouch who likes to see little girls dance. That's the only way to get him to smile. Would you help me get him to smile?"

"Is he sad?" Maya asked.

Amera paused, surprised by the question. She never thought of Curtis being sad or really being anything. "Yes," she lied, deciding to be simplistic.

"Okay."

Amera grabbed a chair and pulled out her cell phone so she could videotape her.

"I'm ready."

"Don't you need music?"

"Nope." Maya stood still a moment then closed her eyes. She slowly opened them then started to dance. She moved to a sound only she could hear, her motions were at times childish and awkward, but her intent was pure and beautiful. She danced with joy and it echoed in every step.

"Thank you," Amera said when Maya stopped and bowed.

"Now it's time for bed," Florence said.

Maya pulled off a bracelet made of pink plastic beads. "Give this to him. I made it."

"It's lovely. Thank you."

"And I--"

"Didn't you hear me? It's time for bed," Florence said.

"It's okay," Amera said taking Maya's hand. "I'll take her. Goodnight." She smiled at her friend then walked Maya upstairs to her room.

Florence's smile quickly disappeared once Amera was out of view. Damn, she didn't need this. Seconds later, she felt, rather than heard, the man who walked up behind her. The man who shared both her business and her bed.

"I thought I told you to cuts ties with that woman," he said.

"It's not that easy."

"We can't have her looking too closely at what we're doing here. We had it good before she--"

Florence turned to him and touched his cheek. He

wasn't a good looking man, but he didn't need to be to please her. They thought alike and had a bond she'd never had with anyone else. "I know. Don't worry, she'll give up soon."

"You said that two years ago."

Florence kissed the hard lines of his mouth. "She won't find anything," she said in a soft purr then flashed her winning smile. "I'm very careful."

She still didn't feel like going home. Amera wandered around the mall thinking about Maya's dance and the gift she'd given her. The thought of the bracelet made her both angry and sad. Curtis wasn't worth it, but Maya didn't know that and the thought of helping someone had made the little girl happy. She'd told Amera that she didn't believe in Santa Clause, but she did believe in magic and that dancing made her feel magical. Amera didn't quite understand what she meant since she'd never believed in such things.

She looked down at the ring on her finger. She really should sell it. It would be a great surprise for Florence and help Peale House. How could she let so much money just sit on her finger? The answer to that question left her mind the moment she collided with a woman glancing down at her phone. Amera hit the woman hard and stumbled back. So did the woman, losing her grip of her cell phone and it clattered to the ground.

"Are you okay?" Or at least that was what she was

about to say, but a man rushed up to the other woman's side first, eager to be her rescuing knight.

"Are you hurt?" he asked, as if he'd come across a trauma victim.

"No," she said with a slight laugh. "It's my fault."

The man helped the other woman to her feet. Amera saw the woman's face and stared amazed--the angel stealer. How could she have met her twice in two days? She picked up the woman's phone and handed it to her. "It's not broken. I'm glad you're all right," she said then started to walk away.

"Wait."

"What?"

"I was sorry about--"

Amera shook her head. "It's okay."

"Please let me make it up to you. Oh look, there's a little coffee shop over there. Wouldn't you like something warm to drink? Come on, my treat," the woman said quickly giving Amera no room to say no.

Moments later, Amera sat in the café holding a cup of black coffee, staring at a woman people seemed to just drift towards like a light. The clerks were extra solicitous, other patrons gestured to an empty table. Amera was used to being invisible, but in the woman's presence, she felt even more so. Susan Pentworth was very chatty--discussing her job as a house stylist, who helps realtors stage houses for sale in great detail--but to Amera's surprise, the fact that she kept talking non-stop, didn't bother her. Susan appeared genuine. "So what do you do?" Susan asked motioning to the plate of cookies and biscotti she'd bought.

Amera shook her head. "I'm an executive assistant."

Susan took her third cookie and bit into it. "I don't know how you can resist. You have better control than I do or..." She began to grin. "Are you trying to keep your weight down until after the wedding?"

"Wedding?"

"Yes, when's the date? Oh wait." She lightly tapped her forehead then rolled her eyes. "I probably should first say congratulations."

"Congratulations?"

"Yes. I didn't see that ring before, trust me I would have noticed a ring that gorgeous, so he must've just proposed."

Amera sighed. "No, I'm not getting married. This is just a joke."

"It's not real?" Susan reached across the table and grabbed her hand. "It certainly looks real."

"The ring is real. It's just..." She shook her head. "It's hard to explain."

"Your boyfriend is playing with your heart?"

"I don't have a boyfriend. I'm single."

"You and I are so much alike."

No we're not, Amera wanted to say. The woman had men flocking to her. She wore fabulous clothes and had an interesting career. She was nothing like her. The poor woman was clearly delusional.

"Isn't it great to make new friends?" Susan continued.

"I could use some help with finishing up my shopping. Want to come?"

She probably needed someone to carry her bags. "Sure," Amera said deciding that a few more hours of shopping were better than going home to her empty apartment. She was quickly pleased with her decision, liking Susan's chatty, happy personality more than she'd expected.

"What do you think?" Susan asked showing Amera a pinwheel hat she'd just put on.

Amera didn't think it was possible, but the hat actually made her look terrible. "Try this," Amera said placing another more suitable hat on her head.

Susan looked in the mirror then her face crumpled into tears.

"What's wrong?" Amera asked.

"I'm just so happy. You're so sweet. I don't have a lot of girlfriends. Actually, I don't have any."

"Well, if you always cry like this, of course you won't."

Susan wiped a tear away. "Women get jealous. They think I'm trying to steal their men."

"I guess I'm safe because there's no man to steal."

She placed the hat back on the stand. "There should be. Let's go."

"You want to steal my man?" Amera asked as they left the store.

"No, that came out wrong. But don't you want to be in a relationship?"

"I barely have the time."

"But if you did?" She spotted a bench and sat down then took out a black book from her handbag. "I have a wonderful man."

Amera sat down next to her. "I thought you said you were single."

"No, I said we were alike."

"But you implied ...."

Susan grinned, then giggled like a naughty girl. "True. I wanted see how you'd react, but you didn't react at all." She pulled out her phone. "Can I show you a picture of my little boy?"

"Sure," Amera said, knowing there was no way she could say no.

Susan pulled up a picture of a little boy dressed up like a train.

Amera smiled. "Cute. Great Halloween costume."

"No, it's not for Halloween. I took this picture two days ago. He wants to be a train when he grows up. The moment he gets home he puts it on." She flipped to another image of the boy with a man in the background. "At least I got him to stop wanting to wear it to pre-school."

"And the handsome man in the background is your husband?"

"Yes, James."

"Let me guess. He's also rich, smart--"

"And he's kind to animals."

Her life just got more and more perfect. Why did she worry about friends when she had a life like this? A healthy family, a job she loved and people who treated her like royalty.

"What do you want in a man?" Susan asked putting her phone away.

Amera shrugged with nonchalance. "The same."

"How about the person who gave you that ring?"

"My boss?"

Susan's mouth fell open. "Your *boss* proposed?"

Amera waved her hand, horrified by the thought. "I told you, it's a long story."

"So you're not interested?"

"Absolutely not. He's not kind, he's arrogant, cold and he only eats animals."

Susan shivered. "Then why do you stay?"

"I like the work. It has its perks. I make good money and get to travel and the days are never the same." Unfortunately, her job would soon end, but she didn't plan to tell Susan that bit of information. "He's a jerk and I don't like him, but...there's something there." Something that made him unlike Bishop Senior. She knew his father would never have donated the food to Peale House, he wouldn't have even looked at the proposal. But that didn't matter now. Any redeeming qualities he had were buried so deep they might as well not exist. "Are you finishing up your Christmas list?"Amera asked, unable to read what Susan was scribbling down.

"Yes, that's it," she said absently. "You devote your life to your work, don't you?"

"I'd like a little romance, but I know it's silly to say,

because it's not going to happen. There's no man in my future."

Susan put her black book away. "You may be surprised. Let's do this again. I'd love to have you over for dinner."

Amera shook her head. "I don't think we can be friends."

Susan's face fell. "Why not?"

"Because I envy you," she said with a reluctant sigh. She didn't want to be honest, but felt she had to. She glanced around the mall, which was decorated with the bright, cheerful colors of the season. "I spoke to a little girl tonight, Maya, who still believes in magic and I envied the joy her belief gave her. All this happiness around us, I can't feel it. I've never felt it. I look at the expression on your face and the connection you have with your family and it's all foreign to me." She bit her lip, ready to reveal something she never had before. "Just once I'd like to see someone's face light up because I entered the room, to have people *I* belong to. But I learned early that there are dreams that can make you strong and other dreams that can destroy you. Yes destroy," she repeated, seeing the shock on Susan's face. "Dreams that make you lie to yourself. Dreams just as toxic as the taste of whiskey to an alcoholic who thinks she can stop after just one drink."

"I don't believe that. Everyone should dream."

Amera flashed a sad smile. "Says a woman who has had all of her dreams come true."

"Not all."

"You don't understand," Amera said standing, ready to leave.

Susan stopped her and shook her head, perplexed. "You act as if having a home and family is impossible for you."

"Because it is. I'm thirty-one years old and I've only loved once and he didn't love me, so I never tried again. Don't be surprised, it wasn't hard. People wonder how I can work with my boss, but I understand him more than most people do. He deals with facts and figures, rather than emotion. I wouldn't know what to do in an environment that was too personal or emotional. So you see, as much as I want it, I wouldn't know what to do with a family. I'm not emotionally equipped. But people like you are and it makes me just as happy but also tears me apart."

Susan sniffed and wiped her eyes. "That's just too sad."

"I'm sorry I didn't mean to make you cry."

"You're not even forty and you're talking as if life and love have passed you by. You have plenty of time and it's never too late to fall in love."

Amera shrugged. "Maybe, but that's why we can't be friends."

"No, that's why we *have* to be friends." Susan pulled out a card and handed it to her. "Please reconsider. I really like you and think we'd be good for each other. You don't have to be alone."

❄

You don't have to be alone. Amera entered her apartment with Susan's words echoing in her mind. Was being alone so wrong? She'd always been alone. One reason she'd shared so much with Susan was because she didn't expect to see her again. She sat in her apartment thinking about the factory workers about to lose their jobs, how she couldn't help Bill, the pink slip on her desk, and Peale House having to turn people away. She had to come up with the perfect way to get back at Curtis. She briefly dreamed about putting salt in his coffee, causing him to miss a major meeting, hijacking his email account and filling it with porn sites or secretly taping one of his nose-bleed episodes and sending it to his father. That thought made her smile. He'd be completely humiliated, but she wasn't sure that act would be bad enough.

She turned on the TV and saw a holiday film, showing a family that reminded her of Susan. Here she was, a single woman thinking about revenge against her boss, while Susan was likely preparing for a holiday party filled with family. How different their lives were.

"Wishing is for wimps," she said to herself then opened up her handbag to toss out Susan's card. Then she saw Maya's pink bracelet. She pulled it out and stared at it for a long moment, in her mind seeing the little girl dancing with joy then giving Amera the gift so that she could make Curtis happy. A man she didn't know.

Amera felt the stinging of tears, the weight of loss--for the workers, for Peale House, for herself--engulfing her in misery. She closed her eyes, covered her face and cried.

CHAPTER 5

*K*yle knew that phones didn't fly, but for a moment he thought they did when one flew into his lap while he was sitting on the couch watching TV. He stared down at the phone then up at his wife, Heidi, with a silent question.

"It's your mother," she mouthed.

Damn, he hadn't even heard it ring. He waved his hands and mouthed "I'm not here," and held the phone out to her.

She took a step back and pointed at him, making it clear that she expected him to answer.

He stood and flashed a grin, one that usually melted her heart. He rested his hands on her shoulder and whispered, "Just cover for me this once."

She folded her arms, her expanding middle making her look extra fierce. "No," she said, then spun and walked away.

Kyle silently swore and watched her leave, wishing

he'd found her as attractive as he used to, then picked up the phone. "Hi Mom."

"What did he say?"

He fell back onto the couch. "What does he always say? Mom, stop doing this to yourself. He hasn't changed and he won't. You have to face that. Give up--"

"He's my son and I'll never give up on him," she said in a curt voice.

"I'm your son too," he said in a soft tone, wishing he could be enough. Why couldn't he and his sister be enough for her? She had the two of them and grandchildren she adored. Sure, this year it would be hard, since his sister had decided to spend time with her husband's family, but his mother would be fine with his. Curtis didn't belong, and he never would. In the past, Kyle had been just as hopeful. He'd believed his mother's warm memories of Curtis, he'd never had any of his own. He had always been a distant figure in his brother's life, at times sending money, but never affection. He'd hope for a chance to really get to know him, but this year that hope had died.

"Kyle," his mother said in a soft tone. "If you knew what he used to be. He was such a loving child."

"He's not a child anymore," Kyle said in a flat tone. "And I'm not going to ask him again," he said, inwardly knowing that for his mother's sake, he probably would.

Camille Carroll heard the pain in her son's tone on the

other end of the line. She didn't mean to hurt Kyle. But she was getting older, and there were so many mistakes she wanted to fix. She regretted the choice she'd made and how easily she'd given up custody to her ex-husband. She had remarried well and created a new, loving family, but there was a hole in her heart that only her first born, Curtis, could fill.

"Okay," she said. "I won't force you," she said then sniffed.

Kyle's tone hardened. "Don't let him make you cry. He's not worth it. He doesn't care."

"I know, that's what hurts. I just wanted this year to be different. I'd do anything to get my son back."

"His father was too powerful to fight. He knows you tried. Don't blame yourself for the man he's become. You have to realize that he's just like his father."

But he wasn't always. She remembered when he used to follow her around the house like a shadow. He used to like to dress up in superhero costumes and pretend to rescue her from villains. Her husband had squashed those playful times fast, with the back of his hand or a belt, forcing Curtis to abandon his childish ways.

"He made a choice not to know us. You did nothing wrong."

Camille gripped the phone. She'd made Kyle believe that, even though she knew it was a lie.

That Thursday, Amera called in sick. She had plenty of

sick leave left and still hadn't come up with her revenge strategy, so she decided to take a day to look over her resume and review her list of references. After retrieving her mail from the lobby, she walked back into her apartment, and tossed it on the table. The diamond ring caught the light and twinkled. She held out her hand and stared at the ring. It was gorgeous. It wasn't like Curtis to be impulsive, but she was glad he had been.

She liked wearing it. She liked the feeling of ownership, even though it would be brief since she didn't plan to keep it. It was nice to imagine being the kind of woman who received such gifts. Her looks were what the western world called exotic, but they were considered ordinary in the small African country, squashed between Gabon and Congo, where she had been born. Her light brown hair and eyes had made her unusual, but she had soon learned how to fit in, and not stand out, whenever she could, by keeping her hair pulled back most of the time, and not wearing makeup to bring attention to herself.

She looked at the ring then rested her hand on her shoulder. "Oh this?" she said to an imaginary companion. "Yes, I was shocked too when he proposed. He even ordered a string-quartet. The honeymoon? I couldn't decide whether I wanted us to go to Milan, Morocco, Maine or Madrid so he's taking me to all four. I know, he's amazing and so considerate." She laughed then caught her reflection in the mirror.

That's when she saw a woman who nobody loved, who nobody remembered. She saw a woman with haunted eyes who had felt the sting of cruelty which had withered her heart. For a moment, she had brief flashes of long dirt roads and a blazing sun, a refugee camp where the flies were fatter than the people. She remembered sitting in a classroom devouring as many books as she could--dreaming of traveling to Ghana, England and Canada, wondering what minced pie tasted like and imagining the sensation of feeling snow and sledding in the winter. She privately dreamed of finding a family like the redheaded girl she'd read about, who lived on Prince Edward Island or being the reluctant pickpocket surviving the streets of London, and finding his rightful inheritance. But she soon learned that there was no grandfather for her to live with in the Swiss Alps, or gracious Uncle who had a secret garden, who would come to her rescue. She remembered when she stopped reading those books. When she stopped dreaming.

She'd learned to depend on herself. She used the excellent education she had received to forge a path away from the horrors of her past. Miss Agatha Wenthrop, the woman who had created the Wenthrop Children's Home, the second orphanage she had been raised in believed in education. It didn't matter that they lived miles away from western civilization, she insisted that the curriculum be equal to those who attended the best schools. When Amera arrived in America as an asylee with permanent residence status, she had no trouble securing a place in a small prestigious college, which was paid for by a scholarship she won.

She frowned down at the ring, embarrassed by her moment of weakness and dreamy, wistful thoughts and tried to pull it off. She didn't need a family. She didn't need a man. She was fine as she was. She may be alone, but she wasn't lonely. She twisted the ring, but it wouldn't budge. She sighed. She'd remove it later.

Amera picked through her mail on the table, not expecting anything interesting. She quickly waded through bills and junk mail then a beautiful envelope caught her eye.

CHAPTER 6

Intrigued, Amera turned the envelope over and studied it. It looked like an invitation. She didn't get invitations. Had it come to the wrong address? She checked the label and saw her full name: *America Blessings Thurston.* Who could it be from? Who knew her full name? She never used her middle name, Blessings. She grabbed a letter opener and swiftly cut open the gold lined envelope. Inside was a handwritten note on expensive parchment paper lined with finely woven lace. She read: *You have been personally selected to join The Black Stockings Society, an elite, members-only club that will change your life and help you find the man of your dreams. Guaranteed.*

The Black Stockings Society? She'd never heard of any such organization. Was it some kind of lingerie club? How had they gotten her name? Why were they inviting her, of all people, to join? She scanned the rest of the note.

Dumped? Bored? Tired of being single? Ready to live dangerously? Then this is the club for you. Guaranteed results! Submit your application today.

Dumped? Well, she'd been dumped from her job, did that count?

Tired of being single? Hmmm. Had Susan given her name to some group to cheer her up?

Ready to live dangerously? She wasn't sure, maybe. She could use a change. She held up her hand again. She wouldn't mind shaking up her life a little, especially since she'd be out of work soon. "Sure. Why not?" she said out loud to no one in particular.

Guaranteed results, huh? She looked at the nominal fee and application. *It wouldn't hurt to try it out.* She got a pen and looked at the enclosed questionnaire. Then frowned with disappointment when she looked at the questions. They reminded her of the silly questions one found in those cheap women's magazines. Asking her how she'd spend her holidays or what she'd eat. She tossed the application down. She was a serious woman. This didn't make sense to her. She stood and changed for bed. She was about to turn out the lights when the sight of the invitation floated in her mind. *Tired of being single? Ready to live dangerously?* Those two questions kept going over and over in her mind and every time the answer was yes. She pushed the sheets back and jumped out of bed.

"I don't know what's wrong with me," she mumbled, as she picked up the questionnaire again. But she was eager to see what would happen. She bit her lip then started to answer the questions.

How would you spend your holidays? She'd love a family holiday. A holiday surrounded by people who cared about her, where she felt she belonged. But she didn't have a family so she knew it was just wishful thinking.

Would you prefer candy canes or gingerbread cookies? Definitely, gingerbread cookies.

What would your ideal man be like? She wished people would stop asking her that. *I don't know.* Really. A good person? She didn't have an ideal. She thought of Curtis standing alone at the hotel window--isolated and distant. She felt sorry for him, although she knew no one else would, and besides, he seemed content with his life. What if he wasn't like that? What if he were different? She bit her lip then quickly wrote: A more human, warm version of Curtis. She wasn't even sure what that meant. She crossed it out. Ugh!!! Florence was right. Curtis was the only man in her life. Why would she even think of him as a possibility? She should think of some celebrity or prominent person she admired instead. But Curtis' name kept coming to her. Annoyed, she hastily wrote: 'A smiling Curtis'. It still didn't make sense, but somehow it sounded right. They probably wouldn't know what she meant since they didn't know who Curtis was, but it was all she could think of.

Amera carefully read the 'sworn' oath. *As a member of The Black Stockings Society, I swear I will not reveal club secrets, I will accept nothing but the best and I will no longer settle for less.* She signed the application, gave her credit card information for the nominal membership fee, then hurried back into the hallway to put the application in the outgoing mailbox.

She called in sick the next day too. Her phone rang, but she didn't answer it. Curtis would be upset, but there was nothing he could do about it. She secretly hoped something disastrous happened forcing him to realize how much he needed her. Her mouth spread into a satisfied grin as she imagined him knocking on her door...

"Curtis? What are you doing here?" she said, surprised by his disheveled appearance.

"You didn't answer your phone."

"I'm taking a sick day."

He frowned. "You don't look sick."

"I'm taking the day anyway." She started to close the door.

"Wait," he said grabbing the handle, his voice cracking with panic. "Don't do that."

"Why not?"

"Because I need you."

She stared at him stunned. "What?"

"I need your help." He shoved his hands in his pockets, his tone heavy with regret. "I was wrong. Nothing is going right without you by my side. I didn't realize it until now. Letting you go was the biggest mistake of my life."

"I don't care. I've already gotten another job offer."

"Tell me who. I'll triple whatever they say."

"No."

He fell to his knees. "Please. Please come back to me,

Em. Give me another chance. I'll give you whatever you want..."

Amera replayed her fantasy throughout the day, sometimes changing the details--once she even imagined him crying, but that was so unlike Curtis she found herself laughing instead. It put her in a good enough mood that she didn't mind her job search and even sketched out a way she could anonymously send Bill money if he needed it.

That Saturday, a medium sized package arrived. Inside the box, encased in a purple satin cloth, were four pairs of different types of stockings, a membership card that read *America (Amera) Blessings Thurston, Member, The Black Stockings Society,* and strict instructions. She read the instructions with particular care.

Welcome to The Black Stockings Society. Your first assignment is to take your membership card to Rejuvenation Spa, where you will ask for the deluxe special. Please set aside plenty of time for this appointment. Once you have gone to the spa you will select and wear one of your stockings to work.

How odd? Why would she need to wear her stockings to work? What did that have to do with meeting the man of her dreams? She glanced down at her watch and decided to call the number provided and make an appointment at the spa. The receptionist answered on the first ring.

"Hello, I'd like to make an appointment for the deluxe special."

"We're really busy due to the holidays, but I can squeeze you in if you'd like."

"Sure."

"Can you get here in an hour?"

"What? You want me to come *today*?"

"Yep, otherwise you'll have to wait until the New Year."

Amera rubbed her forehead. She hadn't planned on doing something like this so soon. Maybe she should just wait.

"Ma'am?"

"Okay, yes," Amera said in a rush. "I'll be there." She gave the receptionist her name then plugged the address in her phone and grabbed her car keys.

She couldn't believe where the spa was located, in a suburb on the opposite side of the city from where she lived. She parked her car then glanced up at the large mansion which had been converted into a total service spa retreat. How did the Society expect her to pay for this? Was she going to get a special discount? She looked at the clock, her hour was almost up. She didn't have time to wonder. She hurried inside then skidded to a stop when she saw Crystal. What was she doing here? Or better yet, why did she have to be here now? She didn't want to see her. She'd wait for the New Year. She'd been reckless and that wasn't like her. She spun around.

"Amera?"

She froze, hearing Crystal's heel clicking closer.

"Amera. Is that you?" Crystal walked in front of her. "It is you! What are you doing here?" Her eyes filled with fear and she glanced around like a scared animal. "Is Curtis having me followed because of the other night?"

"No, I'm not here because of him." She turned and headed for the receptionist desk. Since she had gotten caught, she might as well make the most of it. "I'm here for me."

"Oh," Crystal said confused.

Amera could understand her confusion. They both knew she couldn't afford the place on her salary. Amera waved her hand. "It's something I've saved up for."

Crystal started to reply, then her eyes widened, this time not from fear but shock, her mouth forming a perfect 'o'. "Oh. My God."

Amera frowned. "It's not that incredible."

"You're getting married?"

Amera felt blood drain from her face. The damn ring! She waved her hands and shook her head with a vehemence that almost made her dizzy. "No, this isn't what you think. I couldn't get it off."

Crystal pointed at her and flashed sly grin. "I knew you were the one. You're so brave. He's paying for this, isn't he?"

"No, I told you--."

"Sure." She winked. "No one's to know. They're supposed to think it's real. I get it. But do you think the money's really worth it?"

Amera sighed and spoke slowly. "I'm. Not. Getting. Married. And if I were getting married it wouldn't be to him."

"Right, I won't say a word until it's announced."

An attendant approached Crystal and called her away.

"Your secret's safe with me," Crystal said and gave Amera a knowing wink before she left.

Amera inwardly swore and again tried to take the ring off. It stubbornly refused to move.

"Ma'am can I help you?" An attendant, with enviable smooth skin and long lashes, asked with genuine interest. "Are you looking for someone?"

"No," Amera said wondering if she should warn Curtis about Crystal's assumptions. This was all wrong. But she decided she didn't need to worry. There was no way the two of them would meet.

"If you don't have an appointment, I'm going to have to ask you to leave."

Amera glanced at the clock. Her hour was up. "Right." She turned to leave then the strap of her bag broke and the contents of her purse fell to the floor.

The attendant came from behind the counter and bent to help her then froze when she saw something. "Oh wow." She snatched up the membership card. "You're one of those?"

"I'm sorry?"

"A member. Why didn't you say so? Who are you here to see?"

Amera took the card back. "I don't remember."

"That's okay," the attendant said snatching the membership card back, without appearing rude, then she scanned it with her phone. "You're here to see Dalia. Oh wow, you're getting the works." She called another assistant. "Get her another purse immediately."

"But I--"

"Do you have a particular color or designer you'd prefer?"

"Not really," Amera said confused by the question.

"Then don't worry, we'll take care of everything."

After being given a brand new designer handbag, Amera was ushered into a changing area and provided with a luxurious spa robe and slippers. She settled in quickly. Rejuvenation Spa lived up to its name. While waiting for the stylist to arrive, she was treated to an assortment of herbal teas, sliced fruits and freshly baked pastries.

"Oh, there you are," a tall, willowy woman said as she entered the solarium. "Sorry to have kept you waiting. My name is Dalia." Amera followed her into a private room, where she immediately began assessing Amera's hair. "You have soft, fine hair, I can see why you haven't put a perm in it." Dalia, then spent the next fifteen minutes peppering Amera with questions about what she did, how she liked her hair or didn't, what special events she liked to go to, etc. "I know just what you need," she said with a flourish.

After shampooing Amera's hair, Dalia applied a very gentle relaxer, to make it manageable, and then used a flat iron and curler to style her hair into a sleek, stylish design that allowed Amera's features to be seen. Amera's hair was in good shape, so Dalia didn't have much trouble taming it, but she did have to cut some of the length.

Initially, Amera wasn't sure she wanted to have her hair trimmed. She was used to just pulling her hair back, and based on her strict upbringing at the orphanage, remembered the importance of not using any of her 'womanly' appeal as a distraction. She had never spent time styling her hair, and was totally shocked when she finally looked at herself. She looked stunning! A temporary darker brown color had been applied to her light brown hair, giving the impression of highlights and providing a nice contrast.

Next, Amera was sent to the makeup artist, but not before getting a wonderful facial and full body rub. Niki, the makeup artist, loved working with Amera.

"You're a perfect canvas," she said when she first saw Amera. "I love your bone structure; high cheek bones, full lips, and my, oh my, what do we have here? Light brown eyes. Quite unusual." When Amera had been at the orphanage, she had been called 'white girl' because of her eyes and hair color, and had overheard one of the caretakers refer to her as a product of the 'occupation'. It wasn't until she was older that she came to understand, that at that time, foreigners from Europe had been working in that part of the country and many assumed she was the product of a union between her mother and one of them.

Niki spent the next hour showing Amera how to get a 'natural' look, without using too much or too little make up. Amera liked the basics, and primarily only used an eyebrow pencil to fill in her light brown eyebrows and lip gloss. "Make-up is important to a woman's image," Niki told her. "It says, you care about yourself. That you are a professional." With her new hairdo, Amera was open to all the information Niki shared with her. One makeup trick she showed Amera, was how to give her eyes a subdued smoky look and which lipsticks worked best for her. At the end of the session, Amera left the spa feeling, and looking like a new woman.

Amera stared at her reflection that Monday morning completely in awe of what a spa visit and a great pair of stockings could do. She'd paired the lace patterned stockings she had selected with a dark blue pencil skirt and white blouse. Initially she had felt odd wearing a pair of expensive stockings to work, that wasn't her style. She was used to wearing her uniform. She had a total of ten pieces that made up her work attire: A brown and dark blue tailored suit, two long sleeve tailored blouses, one black sweater dress, two pairs of fitted slacks (brown and blue to match her suit jackets), and one grey wool sweater. She wasn't sure if what she had selected went with the stockings. But she didn't have many other items, so what she selected would have to do. She still hadn't been able to remove the ring, but felt less worried about it. In a week she'd be gone anyway, so if someone asked, she'd just say her boyfriend had proposed. No one could argue that. Besides, somehow the ring seemed to add to her new look. She even felt more confident about getting additional funding for Peale House. She'd left a message for Florence that she wanted to see her and go over the numbers again and fix the proposal.

Amera left her apartment ready for her final week with Curtis. She was ready to put her plan in action. She had decided that she was going to make his life a little hectic for that week, so that he'd regret getting rid of her. She was no longer going to fade into the background.

Once Amera entered the office building, several men held doors open for her, greeted her with 'hello' and a smile when previously they walked past. Amera found the new attention a little disconcerting, but then felt flattered. Maybe, Susan was right. She didn't have to be alone. She walked into her office with a new spring in her step. She saw a box lying by the side of her door that had been delivered to the wrong department. She bent down to pick it up and move it out of the way.

"No, let me help you," she heard a male voice say. The man rushed forward and took the box from her. "I'm Owen, by the way."

She straightened and looked at him. "I know."

He stared at her, stunned, loosening his hold on the box. She caught it before it hit the floor. "Ms. Thurston?" he said in awe, his gaze trailing the length of her.

Amera set the box aside. "Yes, it's me," she said with a nervous laugh. "I know it's a shock."

"It's incredible. I mean, I knew you weren't bad looking, but..." He groaned. "And I should stop talking before I start the beginnings of a sexual harassment suit."

Amera grinned, tucking a strand of hair behind her ear. "No, it's nice."

He blinked and started to grin back. "Now I get it. I knew they said love changes things but I'd never seen a transformation like this."

" Love?"

"Yes. Who's the lucky man?" He nodded to her ring.

She'd briefly forgotten about the ring, but at least now she knew what to say. "He surprised me too."

"Everybody thought Bishop was the only man in your life. I guess we were wrong. You're a sly one," he said playfully nudging her with his arm. "Having another life when a man like Bishop dominates it. I'm happy, but I guess that means we'll soon lose you."

I was already out the door. "I guess so."

"It makes sense. Your fiancé wouldn't want you to work at the same pace you've been working. Available after hours, especially when you can get something better."

Her phone rang.

"Bishop?"

"Of course," Amera said heading to his office.

Owen followed her. "I have to meet this man."

"Because you don't believe me?"

"No, because I need to meet the man who could steal you away from Bishop."

"Hmm," Amera said, then opened the door to Curtis' office.

"I don't care how small the wedding is. I expect an invitation," he said

"An invitation to what?" Curtis asked, not looking up at them.

"Nothing," Amera said.

"Ms. Thurston's getting married," Owen said at the same time.

"Is that right?" Curtis asked, but she could tell by his tone that he knew the truth.

"She's certainly one for keeping secrets. It's amazing, right?" Owen said.

Curtis looked up, made a quick sweep of her new look then held her gaze. "Almost unbelievable," he said, stroking his chin with the lazy motion of a predator.

She glared at him.

"You'd better be nice to her to convince her to stay with us," Owen said.

Amera glanced at Owen confused. Didn't he and others know this was her last week there? Surely word had gotten out about her being let go. But if he didn't know, she didn't plan on telling him.

"Have you met this mystery man?" Curtis asked with a slight raise of his eyebrow.

Owen shook his head. "No."

"Then why would she leave?"

Amera rubbed her fingers together, daring him to mention the pink slip.

Owen's gaze darted between them and he shifted awkward, as if he felt a sudden tension in the room. "I should go."

"Yes," Curtis said, his gaze never leaving Amera's face.

Owen opened his mouth to say something to Amera, then thought better of it and left.

Curtis leaned back in his chair. "So you're getting married?"

"Did you want something?"

"I find it amazing that you succeeded where I failed. Perhaps I should get some advice. How should I go about getting a fiancée?"

"Sir--"

"What persuaded you to say yes? The candlelight or the flowers. Or maybe he did something different."

She folded her arms. "Yes."

"What?"

"He made me want to show up."

It was a low blow and hit its target. Curtis' eyes darkened dangerously, but she stared back with boredom. "Now let's review your schedule for this week."

"Did I get you into trouble?" Owen asked over the phone towards the end of the day.

"No," Amera said staring out at the falling rain, it was too warm for snow. "I know how to handle him."

"I would have loved to see that," he said with a smile in his voice.

Amera bit her lip then said, "Stop by my office before you leave, and I'll give you a brief recap."

"I'll be right there."

Amera hung up the phone then closed her eyes. She really shouldn't do this, but she'd always liked Owen and wanted to tease him. She'd give them both a good laugh.

She opened the top two buttons of her blouse and sat on the corner edge of the desk with her legs crossed. She looked down at her midnight-black sheer, thigh high stockings, with a laced pattern that made her feel bold. She heard his footsteps and grinned. "Come in," she said before he could knock.

Curtis walked in.

Amera gasped in horror and toppled off the desk, landing with a thud. She scrambled to her feet and smoothed down her skirt, her face burning with embarrassment. "Excuse me, sir. I didn't expect--"

He quickly closed the distance between them, and stood close enough for her to smell his cologne, and feel his breath on her skin. "Do you think I haven't noticed the change?"

Amera cleared her throat, wishing he didn't smell so good and annoyed that she even noticed. "Sir, I--"

He lifted her hand and ran his thumb over her ring. "Are you going to make me regret giving this to you?"

Amera opened her mouth to say 'no' then she saw Owen in the doorway, his face a caricature of shock--his eyes bulging and his mouth open. "You didn't give me anything," Amera corrected in a low voice.

"You're actually going to deny it?"

She gripped his hand and lowered her voice even further. "Just this once, don't say another word." She held his gaze then glanced behind him before looking at him again, hoping to make the message clear that they were being overheard.

Curtis stared at her for a long moment, his eyes cold

and insolent. As the seconds slipped passed, she boldly held his gaze, although her heart raced in anticipation. If he ruined this moment for her, she'd certainly make him pay. Then, as if she'd spoken her warning aloud, his dark gaze shifted from ice cold to blazing hot, and her heart started beating fast for an entirely different reason. Soon she not only found the scent of his cologne distracting, but also his nearness.

Finally, he released her hand then looked around the office before grabbing her umbrella from its stand. He mumbled 'thanks' as if that was what he'd come in for then nodded at Owen, before he left.

Amera resisted the urge to follow him, pushing down her strange response to him. Taking her umbrella was a good cover, but she realized that she'd end up getting soaked on her way to her car. Maybe that was his intention--the bastard.

Owen gave a low whistle. "I've never seen that look before." He sat down. "What's going on between you two?"

Amera took a deep breath. She wouldn't be upset and at least he'd allowed her to keep her lie. "It's just work related."

"What I saw didn't look work related."

"You know him. It's always about business."

Owen looked at her unconvinced. "Sure."

Amera waved her hand, trying to make light of the matter. "He's just annoyed that I didn't tell him about my engagement first." She grabbed her coat. "Do you have an umbrella?"

"Sure, why?"

"Since he took mine, do you mind walking me to my car?"

Owen stood up and grinned. "It'll be a pleasure."

Vernon waited in the shadows, glad for the rain. Most people would be inside the building and that would make his job easier. Amera was one problem he had to extinguish fast. He couldn't have her come by and look too closely at their numbers. She could ruin everything for them and he couldn't allow that. Florence was his heart, and he had to keep her safe. Since Amera wouldn't take the hint, he'd have to make his message clear and take her out of the picture.

He saw her distinctive umbrella. He'd seen it many times before and had even commented on it. To him it was as beautiful as a bull's eye the size of a billboard. He couldn't miss. As she walked across the parking lot, he grinned, putting on his silencer. "Don't worry, baby. All our troubles are over," he said, before he lifted his gun and fired.

CHAPTER 7

She'd never shared an umbrella with a man before and realized that she liked it. Actually, to her surprise, she liked Owen. He was a kind, steady, man who took Curtis' abuse with ease. She was about to ask him about his holiday plans when Owen said, "Hey, isn't that your umbrella?"

She looked and saw it blowing past. Had Curtis just thrown it away when he got into his car? Was he really that careless? "Help me grab it," she said. She made a move to run after it when she caught something shiny in the corner of her eye. She turned and saw a watch catching the light of a streetlamp. She moved closer, surprised that a watch would be left on the ground, then stark and vivid fear gripped her when she recognized the watch and the person it belonged to.

She raced over to the lifeless figure lying on the ground, but felt as if she were moving in slow motion.

She didn't seem to be getting any closer to him. She kept expecting Curtis to get up and swear or hold up his head, but he didn't move. He didn't moan or groan. He didn't make a sound. He just lay still. Like a fallen beast. He couldn't be dead. Could he? *Was this how his life would end?* she wondered. She saw the blood on the side of his face and under his head being washed away by the cold rain.

"I got your umbrella and...Mother of God," Owen said staring down at Curtis. "Someone finally did him in."

Amera fell to her knees and checked Curtis' pulse. He still had one. "Call an ambulance."

Owen pulled out his phone. "He had plenty of enemies."

"He's not dead yet," Amera said refusing to refer to Curtis in the past tense.

Owen spoke to the dispatcher then asked Amera, "Is he breathing?"

"Barely." She ripped off her gloves, balled them up then pressed them against the gash on his head.

Blood spread onto her skirt, and stockings, but she didn't care. The wound looked bad. "You're going to be alright," she said, although he didn't look as if he would be. "You wouldn't let your old man out live you, would you?" she whispered in his ear.

She saw his eyelids flutter.

"Yes," she said, encouraged by the motion. He was a fighter. "Just imagine what he'd say."

Curtis groaned and started to move.

"Stay still, the ambulance is coming."

He muttered something she couldn't understand, then he was still again.

The ambulance arrived within minutes and whisked him away, leaving her to talk to the police. She felt helpless because she hadn't seen anything and didn't have much information to help them. Someone had tried to kill him and the saddest part was that if he died, nobody would care.

Thoughts collided together, but didn't make sense. Curtis remembered the sight of a sexy pair of stockings, feeling a sense of unease, seeing a reflection of a man, hearing the sound of a woman's voice, feeling her touch--and not wanting her to leave. He remembered thinking that this was a terrible way to die and that he couldn't let his father out live him. Voices asking him rapid-fire questions he couldn't respond to, telling him things he couldn't understand.

He struggled to reach the surface of his mind, piercing through the fuzzy chaotic, dark thoughts, desperate for a semblance of order. But when he opened his eyes the sense of desperation grew stronger. Something was wrong, but he didn't know what. He didn't even know why. But something ominous weighed heavy on his mind. It was as if his memories were locked in a box for which he didn't have the key to open.

Owen came over to him. "You're in the hospital."

"What?"

"You're in the hospital. You've been unconscious for two days."

He shifted his gaze to the window and saw the sun, now understanding why the room seemed so bright when he'd last remembered the sight of the moon. "What happened?"

"The police are looking into it. You can't remember anything?"

"No."

"Someone shot you. Fortunately, the bullet only grazed you. What did the real damage was the car."

"The car?"

"Yes, you hit your head on it when you went down."

Someone shot at him? Curtis gripped the bed sheets, consumed by rage. Why had someone tried to kill him? He searched his mind to make sense of it, but the words wouldn't come. Instead, in brief flashes of insight, he saw a man he didn't know, a diamond ring. The ring. He felt an overwhelming sensation that something was important to him. No, not something, *someone*. A sudden fear seized him. He wasn't the target, she was in danger, but he didn't know why. "Where is she? How is she? Did she get hurt too?"

"Who?"

Who? Yes, who? She was always by his side. He remembered her eyes, she looked at him without fear. The only person who did. She wore a ring. No, not just any ring. *His* ring. "My wife."

"What?"

"My wife." God, he didn't even remember her name. What was her name? Why did he have the feeling that he never used it? It didn't matter. He had to reach her. "She was there. Is she okay? Where is she?"

"You're confused."

He pounded the bed. Yes, he was confused, but not about this. Something was wrong. Why wasn't Owen telling him? "Tell me where she is."

"I'll be right back."

Curtis grabbed his wrist. "Are you going to get her?"

"Yes, sure, of course," he said, his words running into each other, almost sounding like gibberish.

Curtis relaxed his grip and sat back feeling drained but relieved, that meant she was alive. "Good."

"He appears to be suffering from transformative-retrograde amnesia," the doctor told Owen as the two of them stood in the hallway. Kyle wasn't there when his brother regained consciousness, but had come to visit. His mother stayed away, after initially seeing him that first day, when he was in a coma. Owen would call Kyle later to let them know the prognosis.

"What does that mean?"

"The good news is that his long term memory is intact, but his short term memory has been affected."

"Affected? It's been destroyed, doc," Owen said with

feeling. "He thinks he has a wife and he's never been married."

"Are you sure about that?"

"I would have known, I think," he said, suddenly unsure. "But I don't know her name and he acts as if I should."

"Be patient with him and I'm sure you'll get some clues to her identity."

"When will he be okay?"

"This could last a week or month. I think he'll be fine with rest. He just can't take major shocks."

Owen swore and paced. What was he going to do? Amera would know. They'd taken turns looking in on him. They'd been able to keep the media away, but he didn't know for how long. Fortunately, Amera was always calm and clear headed and he needed that right now. "He's awake," Owen said, once she answered the phone. "But there's a problem. The last several weeks are gone from his memory."

"Oh no."

"But that's not the worst part," Owen said with a heavy sigh.

"It gets worse?"

"He's asking for his wife."

Amera paused. "His what?"

"I know, that's what I said. I know he's briefly delusional, but of all the things to imagine, why a wife? As if any woman would want to marry him."

"What do you want me to do?"

"You're good with him. You can help him clear his

thoughts. Talk to him, find out who she is. I've never seen him so agitated. He's really worried about this imaginary woman, as if he truly cares for her. To be honest, seeing him so human is a little scary."

Amera sighed. "I'll be right there."

There was definitely something wrong with his face. Amera stepped into Curtis' hospital room with caution, analyzing his features with amazement. His face hadn't been disfigured or anything and others would say it was fine, a slight bruise and cut, the stitches hidden on the side of his head, but nothing more visible. However, Amera knew it was all wrong. It wasn't Curtis' face. Instead of the biting black stare she'd grown used to, she was greeted by dark brown eyes that looked relieved by the sight of her. He had never looked relieved before. He was too reserved for such an expression. Owen had said he'd recover from the head injury, but was there more damage than they thought?

Amera pushed her shoulders back. She wouldn't pity him, he didn't need that. If he was to recover, he needed to be treated like the man he used to be. "Couldn't you have found another way to gain sympathy?" she said in a curt tone.

Curtis seized her hand. "Thank God you're okay."

Amera was too startled to reply. Not just by his words, but by the swift, powerful attraction that engulfed her as his large hand swallowed hers. She'd been with him many times before and never felt such a visceral reaction. Her eyes dropped to his full bottom lip, her skin feeling the heat of his hand causing a tingling pit in her stomach. What was wrong with her? She started to draw her hand away, but he tightened his grip, but not enough to her hurt.

"It's okay, you don't have to be afraid," he said in a tender tone.

Her heart picked up speed, her body longing to move closer. He'd lost his mind, and clearly so had she. "Wait. What?"

Curtis looked down at her hand. "I don't know what I would have done if something happened to you."

" Uh...Sir--."

Curtis frowned. "Why are you calling me that? And you're trembling. What's wrong?"

He'd never looked or touched her like this before. He was ill, she had to be the rational one. She had to deal with the facts. That was the language Curtis understood. She swallowed and kept her tone businesslike. "You were--"

"Shot. I know, but you don't have to worry. I'm okay."

"No, you're not. You've suffered a major head trauma and you've lost some memory."

He rested his head back and closed his eyes. "I'm so tired."

"You need to rest."

"I'm sorry, I can't remember, but I'll keep you safe."

He never apologized. And why did he need to keep her safe? She pressed her free hand to his forehead. Was he running a fever?

He frowned. "You're still trembling."

She yanked her hand away.

His dark eyes met hers. "Don't you believe that I can protect you?"

The hard gaze and tone were reminiscent of the old Curtis, even though his words didn't make sense. "Of course. I just never thought I'd see you like this," she said, holding his gaze when she really wanted to look away.

"I'm going to make him regret the day he pulled that trigger."

Amera cleared her throat wondering when he'd let her hand go. It was becoming distracting. "You have to rest first, sir--"

He gritted his teeth. "I wish you'd stop calling me that."

"But I--"

His brows drew together. "Work for me," he finished. He slowly nodded his head as if some pieces were coming together. "At the office."

"Yes, you know me from the office. That's where we met. You hired me. Do you remember that?" she asked with a note of cautious hope.

"Yes, of course I do."

"So you remember the business you're in and the role you play?"

"Yes, yes," he said irritated. "I know all that, but..." He rubbed the back of his neck. "There are a lot of things I don't remember." He swore. "Things I should." He sighed. "Does father know about us?"

"No and--."

"How are you handling the media?"

"We're trying to contain it as much as possible."

"Good. Any sign of weakness..."

"Makes you fresh prey." She finished.

He nodded grimly. "You know my father well."

"And I know you too and I think--."

"Have the police found anything?" he asked.

"They're looking into it."

His brow rose a fraction in disappointment. "You know I don't like vague responses."

"So, whoever shot you is like a ghost. He wasn't caught on any of the cameras, but it's still early."

"The 48 hour window is closed," Curtis said in a grim tone.

"But they'll keep the case open. Now you can hardly keep your eyes open. You need to rest."

"Hmm."

She turned to leave, hoping the motion would encourage him to let her hand go.

He kept his grip on her wrist and tugged her to him. "You're just going to leave?"

"Yes."

"Without even a kiss goodbye?"

A kiss? This was proof he was insane! Amera briefly thought of slapping him. She'd thought of doing so many times before, but she couldn't. Especially when he was looking at her with such a trusting brown gaze. Plus, he'd suffered enough head trauma. But she couldn't kiss him, *could she?* Maybe a kiss could shock him back into his senses. He never displayed affection. He'd likely be disgusted. Disgusted was good. Amera fought back a grin before she pressed her lips against his. She'd intended for it to be a little awkward and sloppy, but somehow Curtis adjusted his head and mouth and turned her attempt into something warm and delicious.

Soon she felt like she was sinking into sweet, melted caramel and felt as hot as a flame. She quickly drew away, the heat of confusion and arousal burning her face. She felt mortified. She'd kissed him, but somehow he'd ended up kissing her. It had been a stupid strategy, even if it did shock him from his amnesia. She stared at him, ready for the dark look of distaste, but another dark look entered his gaze. One filled with a savage rage.

"I'll catch him," Curtis vowed. "And make sure you're never this frightened again."

Amera nodded her head, almost crying in delight when he released his grip. She didn't fear his imaginary enemy, the one he thought had threatened their lives. She'd worked for him for five years and witnessed his mercurial moods and temper, but she'd never seen him as a man before. Now that was all she could see--the magnificent size of him, the amazing breadth of him, the astounding beauty of him. And for the first time in five years, she feared him.

His face changed, but she couldn't read the expression. He pushed the sheets away and swung his legs over the side.

"What are you doing?" she asked.

"We're leaving. I can see the fear in your eyes. You're not telling me something."

"You're not going anywhere," she said pushing him back before he could stand. "They have to observe you a few more days."

"I can sign a waiver. Let's go." He stood too fast. His lips grew white, his face pale before he pitched forward. She caught him and stumbled under his weight. He wore only a hospital gown, so she could feel every part of him, pressed against her, with intimate accuracy. She swallowed hard and managed to push him back onto the bed.

She called him a few names under her breath as she lifted his legs and settled him back against the pillows. She wiped sweat from her forehead and struggled to get her breathing back to normal. Why did his body have to feel so hot and heavy? Why did her body seem to like it? She shook her head. She had to get out of there.

"What happened?" he asked, sitting up, then wincing.

"You need to be careful," she said adjusting his pillow. "You fainted."

He stared at her alarmed. "No, I didn't." He tugged on his hospital gown. "I probably tripped on this stupid thing."

"It doesn't go to the ground."

He narrowed his eyes. "You're enjoying this, aren't you? I look like an idiot. I want--"

"Your pajamas and slippers. I know."

"Not the--"

"Fine knit cotton blend, but the silk ones."

A small smile touched the corner of his mouth and respect entered his gaze. "You do know me well, but of course you would."

Yes, she would. She'd helped him pack for business trips many times. But she knew telling him so wouldn't make a difference.

He reached for her hand again, she moved it out of reach. He looked at her confused. "I've disappointed you that much that you won't even let me touch you?"

"It's not you," she lied. "It's...I'm still in shock. I was the one who found you. I was the one who cradled your head and watched your blood soak through my gloves. I had to talk to the police and admit that I didn't know anything. If you know me at all, you know that I hate not being able to do something. You've been unconscious for two days, while Owen and I did as much damage control as possible. I'm exhausted and I just want to go home."

"You're right. Everything is like a fog, but I never considered all that you've had to go through. I'll make it up to you. Go home and rest."

Amera stood frozen for a moment. She'd expected an argument not his compassion. "Thank you si--uh--Curtis," she quickly corrected when she saw his jaw tighten. Saying his name felt awkward on her tongue, but she stumbled over it and pasted on a smile, eager to leave. "Bye."

"Well?" Owen asked when Amera came out of Curtis' hospital room.

"You're right it's bad," Amera said, fighting to keep her voice steady. She tugged on her blouse wishing she didn't feel so hot.

"He still thinks he has a wife?"

"Yes."

"Who?"

She cleared her throat. "Me."

Owen's brows shot up. "*You're* his wife?"

Amera shook her head. "No, he *thinks* I'm his wife."

Owen nodded looking pensive.

Amera frowned. "This is the part where you burst into laughter."

He slapped his forehead. "Of course. Now it makes sense." He grinned. "You were keeping it a secret."

"There is no secret."

"I overheard you talking about the ring. He gave it to you."

"As a joke."

"Bishop doesn't joke."

"He did that night."

"So he proposed at night?"

"He didn't propose. It was just after dinner--"

Owen's eyes widened. "You had dinner with him?"

Amera held up both hands. "It's nothing, but a long boring story that--."

"It's okay. I know what happened. You had to keep it

from his father right? So you had a secret marriage and you were going to pretend that you were just engaged so that--"

She hit him on the shoulder. "I am *not* his wife."

"Then why does he think you are?"

She tapped the side of her head. "Because he's suffered major head trauma."

"But he thinks you are. Just play along for a couple of days."

"I can't do that," Amera said in a sharp tone, trying not to remember his kiss, even though her burning lips wouldn't let her forget. "I can't even go back in there."

"You have to. You may be able to find out who did this. We both know it wasn't random."

"I know."

"But even if someone tried to knock him off, we'd have a hell of a time finding out who. Everybody hates him and a lot of people would be happy to see him gone."

She sighed. "I know."

"You'd have a list of suspects the size of a dictionary."

"I know."

"You'd have an easier time finding someone who didn't *want* to kill him."

Amera held up her hand and glared at Owen. "Shut up."

"Right. Sorry." He made a motion of zipping his lip, but couldn't keep his mouth closed long. "But this could work for you. As his wife you can stay by his side and look out for him, see if anything in his life or anyone is acting strange. He trusts you. There are no major deals coming up, so his schedule won't be a problem. Maybe you can get him to stay hidden for a while and I'll take care of the rest."

"No."

"Why not?"

Amera folded her arms. "I cannot pretend to be his wife."

"Do you know the power you now hold?"

"Power?"

"Yes. Curtis Bishop is a grade-A bastard with memory loss. What if there are things his executive assistant couldn't get him to do that his wife can?"

Amera bit her lip, tempted at the thought. Owen was right. Curtis wouldn't remember his plan for closing the factory or refusing her proposal. Or even, that he had fired her. What if over the next several days she could change his mind and get what she wanted? The words *Ready to live dangerously?* popped in her mind. Was this how things were to go? She'd ruined her first pair of stockings, tearing them on the pavement and getting blood on them while helping Curtis, but she couldn't believe her luck. This was her chance to make this beast human again, before it was too late. It would be a bold action, but she was ready to take the risk.

"What if his memory comes back?"

"The doctor believes the short term ones are gone for good. You could do a lot and get away with it, Ms. Thurston."

Amera folded her arms and stared down at the ground. He was going to get rid of her anyway and if she could do some good in the process, it would be worth it. With Owen's help she could pull it off, at least for a few days or weeks, then pick a fight with him and ask for a divorce. She'd deal with the consequences when the time came, but for now a prime opportunity had fallen in her lap. She looked at Owen then wiggled her fingers, letting her ring sparkle. "Hello, Mrs. Bishop."

CHAPTER 9

Nobody had come looking for him yet. Vernon sat in his bedroom and polished his boots as if nothing else mattered, although he'd been on edge for days. Damn, he'd messed up bad. He'd nearly smashed something when he learned that he'd hit Bishop instead of his intended target. The police weren't giving out much information, but at least he wasn't dead. That would have been a waste. He didn't like killing people when they weren't a threat. He considered trying again, but it was too soon and security would be on alert.

He hoped the incident would still work in their favor. With Amera distracted, she wouldn't look too closely at them. And if she did, he'd know what to do, and this time there would be no mistake.

Amera sat in her car in the hospital parking lot, staring

down at Susan's card. She needed her help, but didn't know how to ask her. She could still see Owen's excited and eager expression after she'd agreed to their plan.

"You leave the logistics to me," he said. "He has another day in the hospital. I'll move your clothes and other necessary items into his place and let the staff know."

"I can do that myself."

Owen shook his head. "A Bishop wife never does any heavy lifting. You might as well get used to some perks, since it won't last long. Of course, I'll need a copy of your key and a list of anything special you want."

"Okay, that's what'll need to be taken care of on the home front. What about the office?"

"Keep him away from the office. He still needs to recover. He can work from home. Hell his father does, it shouldn't be hard to convince him to do the same." He winked and smiled. "Wifey."

Amera frowned. "Don't call me that."

His smile fell. "Sorry. Anyway, I'd give yourself a week, maybe two. Any holiday family gatherings we need to worry about?"

"This is Curtis, remember?"

"I was talking about you."

"Oh, no. None."

Amera still remembered the passing look of pity that had crossed Owen's face. She stared down at the card. She didn't need pity. She needed help and Susan was the only person she could think of to help her really pull off the role.

"Danger, here I come," she said to herself as she dialed Susan's number.

"Hello?" Susan answered on the first ring.

Amera hesitated partly hoping to be able to leave a message. "I'm sorry to bother you but I don't...I mean..."

"It's great to hear from you."

"Uh...thanks."

"What's wrong?"

My boss thinks I'm his wife and I want to fool him by playing that role. "Sorry, I shouldn't have bothered you."

"Let's get lunch." Susan gave her the address. "My treat. See you in an hour." She hung up before Amera could say no.

Amera smiled, knowing she hadn't planned to.

More than an hour later, the two women sat in a private booth in one of the finest Caribbean restaurants in the area. The waiters and waitresses wore colorful outfits, and were extremely friendly, providing Amera and Susan with instant service the moment they sat down. The interior of the restaurant consisted of a mural that was painted on all four walls, depicting the ocean, palm trees and a setting sun. The surrounding helped calm some of Amera's anxiety.

"So what can I do for you?" Susan asked.

Amera rubbed her forehead. "I don't know how to ask you this."

"Just say it fast."

"Ineedyoutoshowmehowtobeawifeforafewdays."

Susan blinked. "Okay, that was *too* fast. Try again just a little slower."

Amera took a deep breath then said, "I need you to show me how to be a wife for a few days."

"A wife?"

"Yes, I know it sounds crazy, but it's something I have to do."

"Why?"

"It's for a good cause."

"Charity?"

Amera tried not to laugh. Curtis certainly wouldn't like to be considered a charity case. "Something like that."

"It's easy."

"Not for me. I've never been in a relationship with a man, except for business, and I don't know where to start."

"What about the one person you loved?"

"That was different and a very long time ago," Amera said, embarrassed that she'd even mentioned it.

"Well, first you have to know what kind of wife you want to be."

Her eyes widened. "There are different types?"

"Of course. Women become wives for many different reasons. And marriages come in different flavors: open marriages, sexless marriages, childfree marriages..."

Amera thought for a moment then said, "I'm in a sexless marriage of convenience."

"Why?"

"Why?"

"Yes, why did you say yes? Then we'll know the role

you need to play. Is he a rich older man nearing his grave with adult children to contend with?"

"No, his father wants him to get married."

"So, it's for image?"

"Yes."

"Then it shouldn't be that hard. I'm sure he has staff that will keep their ears and mouths closed and you'll just attend functions together. Smile, lightly touch his sleeve every once in a while, make him feel smart and successful."

"But I don't have to, he already is."

"A man can never feel too successful."

"But what do I do when I'm alone with him?"

Susan narrowed her eyes. "There's something you're not telling me."

Amera looked out the window and let her shoulders droop. She had to be honest. She turned back to Susan and said in matter of fact tone, "My boss suffered a major head trauma, and has some sort of amnesia and now thinks I'm his wife."

"Oh."

"Oh? Why doesn't anybody see this as funny?"

"I think it's kinda sweet."

"Curtis Bishop is anything but sweet." *Except when he kisses me, which shouldn't have happened and I shouldn't keep thinking about it.* "But he's not himself, he keeps wanting to hold my hand," Amera said determined not to tell her about the kiss. "Is that normal?"

"Depends on the man."

"I've never seen him this way. Crystal, his ex-girl-friend, who was too afraid to even show up for his proposal, probably knows, but I can't go to her. This is beyond my skill set, I don't know what to call him. I've called him 'sir' for so many years that calling him 'Curtis' feels unnatural. The word gets caught in my throat. And I don't know how to look at him

anymore or---"

"How long have you known him?"

"Five years."

"What kind of wife do you see him with?"

"A cool, sophisticated beauty who travels a lot to keep as much distance from him as possible. They have separate beds and separate lives."

Susan nodded. "Then be that woman."

Yes, I could do that, Amera thought feeling relieved. She was panicking for no reason. He didn't need a lovey-dovey wife, just a showpiece. An accessory, available when necessary. He wouldn't expect anything more. He wasn't that kind of man. The man lying in the hospital bed with the vulnerable eyes and soft mouth was *not* Curtis, but a wounded man under heavy medication. Once he was out of the hospital, she knew what to do and she was ready for her new role.

Owen had to stop himself from whistling as he walked down the hospital corridor that night. A hospital was not the place to be in such a good mood, although the holiday lights and decorations seemed to glow even brighter. It was going to be fun to see what Amera would do. He glanced down at the pajamas Bishop had wanted, he could have had someone else send them, but he wanted to deliver them himself. Seeing Bishop this disoriented had become amusing.

Owen walked into Curtis' room surprised to find the bed empty. Instead he found Curtis standing by the wall. "Are you sure you should be up?"

"I'm fine."

"I came to drop off your things. Your wife will pick you up tomorrow."

Curtis spun around, sending Owen a look that sent chills through him. "My what?"

CHAPTER 10

"Your...wife," Owen said, his voice involuntarily rising in a question.

Curtis frowned.

Owen softly swore, gripping his hands. "Your memory is back?"

"Not all of it, but I certainly remember I don't have a wife."

Owen took a step back. He had to call Amera right away and warn her.

"Wait," Curtis demanded walking towards him. "That was real? It wasn't just a dream?"

"What?" Owen asked taking another step back.

Curtis pointed to a chair. "Sit."

Owen hurried over to the chair and sat.

Curtis folded his arms. "Brief me."

"You have to understand that she did this because she was worried about you and at first--"

"Did I ask for a prologue? I said fill me in."

"You woke up asking to see your wife, when you saw Amera you thought it was her so she decided to... you know..."

Curtis lay on the bed and clasped his hands behind his head. "Be my wife."

"Yes."

"Why is that so hard to say?"

Owen forced a laugh. "Because I know you'd never choose her."

He let his arms fall. "Yet you went along with it."

"For your sake."

Curtis nodded. "What was your plan?"

"It doesn't matter now."

"Tell me."

"She'd take you home and help you rest until your memory returned."

"Who else knows?"

"Just us. Your mother stayed with you the first night."

Curtis stiffened. "My mother came? You told her?"

"She had a right to know--"

"She gave up her rights years ago. Who else did you invite to laugh over my body? My brother too?"

"We thought you might not make it."

"Thought or hoped?"

Owen wisely ignored the question. "The moment you were conscious, they didn't come back."

"And my father?"

"We kept him abreast of your status."

Curtis' gaze sharpened. "Did you tell him that I thought Em was--"

"No," Owen said quickly. "We knew you wouldn't want him to know or anyone. I told you it was just us. We were thinking of your best interests."

Curtis flashed a cruel smile. "You're a terrible liar." He pointed at him. "Mentally, I was as helpless as a lamb and you were ready to lead me to the slaughter."

"No, she was--is--very worried about you and I wanted to help her."

Curtis opened his mouth to make a caustic remark, when a series of memories flooded his senses. He remembered Amera trembling, the look of fear on her face, the tone of her voice as she described her blood soaked gloves that she'd pressed against his head. "Her umbrella."

"What?"

The image of it came and went without revealing its significance. He gripped his hand into a fist. "There's something important I have to remember."

"Let me call Ms. Thurston and tell her that--"

"No. Don't tell her anything."

"But--"

Curtis squeezed his eyes shut and swore. *I have to keep her safe.* "I have my reasons."

Owen nodded slowly, clearly concerned about Curtis' sanity.

Curtis tapped the side of his head. "There's something about that night that's trapped in my mind, but I can't reach it. She's the key to something important, but I don't know what."

"But couldn't you just tell her--"

"No," Curtis said, in no mood to explain himself. He didn't like feeling inadequate. He didn't like not having the answers. He pulled on his lower lip then stopped, the memory of a kiss coming back to him. The feel of Amera's warm, wet mouth pressed against his. The scent of her skin, a feeling of possessiveness consuming him. Had he really liked it that much or had he just imagined liking it? He'd have to find out.

Owen shook his head. "I don't think this is a good idea."

It's all I can think of. "It's just for a few days. You work with her and make this charade work and let me worry about the rest. Make her job as seamless as possible."

"What about your father?"

"I'll deal with him when the time comes. I'm trusting you to keep this between us."

"Right."

"I don't want you to warn her in away. I'll know if she's changed."

"Right."

"Because if you do tell her, I'll redefine the word bastard in ways you could never imagine."

Owen set his glass on his coffee table, while the melodic voice of Judy Garland singing "Have Yourself A Merry Little Christmas" floated through the room. He sniffed at the irony of her words. This was going to be the worst Christmas ever. He shifted his gaze to the bottle of Scotch he'd almost depleted and rubbed his blurry eyes, feeling miserable. He hadn't been able to sleep. Amera was in danger and there was nothing he could do about it. It was all his fault. He never should have encouraged her to pretend to be Bishop's wife. Now he couldn't even warn her. She'd thought she'd be able to manipulate him and instead she was the one being manipulated.

Owen lifted the Scotch bottle to pour himself another glass then stopped as a thought struck him. Unless *he* was the one being manipulated. He set the bottle down, his fuzzy thoughts slowly becoming clear. What if this was all just a cover-up? Bishop had truly sounded worried about her. Bishop never worried about anybody. And his response had been strange when Owen mentioned that Bishop would never have chosen her as a wife. He drummed his fingers on his knee. There was something going on between them. There had to be. He'd seen them in the office--the lowered voices and hushed tones, the secret guarded looks.

He snapped his fingers. Yes, there was definitely something there. Maybe Bishop had let the truth slip and now was trying to cover it up by lying. Bishop didn't want his father to know, that definitely meant he was protecting Amera from something. Bishop only protected things that were important to him. Owen sighed then smiled, feeling his misery disappear. A secret romance. That's what they were trying to hide. He didn't have to worry about Amera anymore, she would be okay. He'd help them both with their little charade until they were ready to let everyone else know the truth. He was a sucker for a happy ending.

Owen lifted his glass as if offering a toast. "Don't worry you two. Your secret's safe with me."

This was going to be easy, Amera thought as she sat in the back seat of the car with Curtis. Getting him discharged from the hospital had been quick and efficient and except for a light, quick, unexpected kiss she was still trying to recover from, he hadn't tried to hold her hand or be near her. She fought to get her warring thoughts under control. In the cold, harsh light of a brand new day she tried to only see the implacable man she'd known for years. She had the schedule all set. She'd already told the kitchen staff to prepare a light lunch. Once he was home, she'd let him rest then casually mention her proposal again, just to get it out of the way.

Her phone rang just as she was silently rehearsing what she would say. She frowned at the number. It belonged to Bill Homer at the factory. "Hello?"

"You have to come quick. There's been an accident at the factory."

"All right. I'll be right there." She hung up then spoke

to the driver. "Change of plans. We have to go to Valdan. Please call the kitchen and let them know to hold lunch."

"Why?" Curtis asked.

"There's been an accident. Bill wasn't more specific."

Curtis held out his hand. "Give me the phone."

"Why?"

"Because you haven't given me mine back yet."

"It was broken."

"It doesn't take this long to get a replacement."

"I planned to give you one at home."

Curtis wiggled his fingers with impatience. "I said give me your phone."

"Why?"

He narrowed his eyes. "You know why."

"I've told you what you need to know."

"You know I like specifics. I'm not going to have us driving all the way there for no reason."

"We have to see what's going on."

"No we don't." He spoke to the driver. "Head for home."

"Keep going," Amera corrected.

"I said go home."

"Ignore him."

"You'll listen if you want to keep your job," Curtis said.

Amera sighed, seeing the confusion on the driver's face in the rearview mirror. "Pull over. I'll get out. You take him home and I'll get a taxi."

"Just give me the damn phone so I can talk to Homer."

"He's stressed enough, he doesn't need you barking at him. Plus, you need to stay as calm as possible. Thanks," she said when the driver pulled to the curb.

Curtis grabbed her wrist and said in a soft voice, "You're not going to win this."

He was right. He was stronger and he'd hold on until he got his way. She glanced at the clock, precious minutes were ticking away. "We don't have time for this."

He held out his other hand. "Give me the phone."

She sighed, then handed the phone to him.

"Get going," he told the driver.

"Where to?"

"The factory," he said as he dialed.

Amera kept her face turned toward the window. Handling him wouldn't be as easy as she'd hoped. He seemed a lot more like the Curtis of before, but he treated her as his wife. The light kiss he'd greeted her with in the hospital still made her lips tingle. But that didn't matter if she had no affect on him. They'd had their first battle and he'd won hands down. She should probably give up on the idea of changing him.

Amera glanced down at her stocking clad legs. Now her second pair of stockings was going to waste. She'd followed the instructions she'd received with the package, and matched this new pair of limited edition, pale blue, opaque geometric inspired boot tights, with her white tailored blouse, and a brown skirt. She had even gone out of her way, and purchased a pair of black leather ankle boots, to match. But now she wished she hadn't gone through the effort. She had wanted to look the image of the sophisticated, cold wife of a tycoon, wearing the most expensive outfit she had in her closet, and she had received glances from every other man, except him. He didn't even appreciate the effort, but that was nothing new. She glanced at him. He wouldn't miss her if she disappeared. She decided, once he was back home, she would lie and say she had to visit family and then never return.

Amera tugged on a button on her coat. Yes, that was it. Her job was almost over anyway. Unfortunately, right at this moment Owen was having all her things moved into the guestroom. After they visited the factory, she'd stay one night then have everything moved out. She briefly thought of still trying to get money for Peale House and helping the factory stay open. She sighed, feeling her heart twist, now she knew her plan wouldn't work.

She heard Curtis end his conversation with Bill, but when he handed her back her phone she didn't ask what it was about. She'd find out when she got there.

"It's a kid."

Amera looked down at her hands. She didn't want to know. She really didn't want to talk to him right now.

"One of the worker's children is caught in one of the machines."

Amera turned to him alarmed, forgetting to be uninterested. "Oh, no."

"There shouldn't be any children there in the first place. They know the rules."

"The mother probably couldn't afford daycare. She

probably was trying to save as much as she could, before the factory closed."

"That's the excuse Homer gave."

"It was an accident."

"Fortunately, we won't be liable if the child dies."

Amera stared at him horrified.

"You think I haven't seen something like this before? I've seen people chop off limbs and fake grievous injuries to get coverage. I've witnessed people sacrifice their children for a little extra cash. Just three months ago, a worker at one of our plants overseas, tried to claim that their child had been born lame from exposure to something its mother had come in contact with while working in the factory. Since no other worker ever experienced the same outcome, we were able to win. Why do you think we have lawyers?"

"The workers at Valdan are not like that."

"How do you know?"

"Because I've seen the data. This factory is one of the highest performing, highly skilled group you have. I don't think anyone there would risk a child's life to get back at you, especially during the holidays."

Forty minutes later they arrived to a scene in chaos-- firefighters fought to free the child, EMTs stood by, workers stood huddled in groups off to the side. Bill Homer walked towards them, sweat pouring down his face, blood on his shirt, but halted when he saw Amera. He looked startled by her changed appearance.

Amera rushed up to him. "You're hurt."

He blinked at her then glanced down. "No, this isn't

my blood. I heard the cries of the child and sprang into action. I was able to get some of the bleeding to stop."

Amera nodded in understanding. "You responded as a physician."

Bill paused, surprised by her statement. "Yes, in my former life. How did you know that?"

Amera inwardly swore. That was information she hadn't meant to let slip. "I...think you mentioned it once."

"What happened?" Curtis asked.

Bill jumped as if he'd forgotten the younger Bishop was there. He wiped his forehead. "Somehow he got his hand caught in one of the machines."

"Will he be okay?" Amera asked.

"Depends. They are still trying to free him. We'll have to wait and see." He turned back to the firefighters. "Let me go see if they need any more information about the machines."

"I'll go with you," Amera said not giving Curtis a chance to stop her.

He could feel their hatred. Their blame. Their gazes hitting him like hard stones. Curtis leaned against a wall and watched the scene. He knew he could return to his car, but he didn't want to leave Amera alone. He didn't like how she'd run to Bill, as if they had a special relationship. He'd never noticed her being so attentive to him before. But he hadn't noticed a lot of things, now he couldn't stop. He couldn't stop watching Amera's lips when she talked, imagining the feel of them against his, and all over him. He noticed the dainty shape of her ears, the bright gleam in her eyes, the way her hips moved when she walked and her legs, he'd never paid attention before.

His fierce attraction to her was a distraction he didn't want, but something he couldn't escape. He saw Amera looking at Bill with intense interest and jealousy tightened its hold around him. He wanted her to look at him like that--only him. But he couldn't think about that right now. A child's life was in danger and he was eager to know the outcome, although he was careful to keep his expression guarded.

He caught the eye of one of the workers, who looked at him in disgust before turning away. He'd felt the workers' animosity before, but it had never fazed him. He'd been taught not to care, but now every piercing, darting look seemed to cut him. It wasn't his fault. He didn't owe them anything. They'd get work elsewhere.

"Mr. Bishop, sir?"

Curtis turned and saw a thin, young man holding his rumpled cap in his hand. "Yes?"

The young man gripped his hands together then fell on his knees. "Please don't bring charges against my sister for what she did." He lowered his head. "We know it was wrong, but she won't be able to survive if you do."

Curtis frowned, disturbed by the sudden emotion that gripped his heart. "Get up."

"Please. We're so sorry," the young man said, his voice choked with tears. "Money was so tight this month and with us soon losing our jobs we were desperate to save some."

Curtis bit the inside of his cheek, wishing that as he looked down at the young man's bowed head, he could see a cockroach like his grandfather or a grasping rat like his father, but all he could see was a young man pleading for his family. "Fine," he said in a curt tone.

The young man nearly collapsed in gratitude. "Thank you, sir." He stood up then winced and lost his balance.

Curtis reached out and grabbed him before he fell. "What's wrong with you?"

"Sorry, sir, old war wound. But I'm getting better." He nodded his head. "Thank you again, sir."

Curtis nodded, then watched the young man limp over to a young woman, speak to her for a few moments before they embraced. He wondered how old they were, and which war the young man had fought in. The wound couldn't be that old if he was so young. And why were they so worried about getting jobs? *Cockroaches know how to survive*, his grandfather always used to say. *Don't feel too sorry for them, they'll turn around and stab you in the back.* Curtis lowered his gaze. Why couldn't he believe that statement right now? Why did he hope that the child survived intact? That the young man's leg healed completely? That the young woman find another job? Their lives were none of his business. *There are winners and losers.* His father's voice echoed in his mind. *Domination is always about destruction.* Did it always have to be? He remembered the look of horror on

Amera's face when he mentioned the possible death of the child. He'd felt that horror as a child, but it had been beaten out of him.

His head shot up when he heard the crowd cheer. A firefighter pulled the child free and raced over to a waiting ambulance. He breathed a sigh of relief then gripped his hand into a fist. He couldn't afford to care. Besides, no one expected him to.

"I'm not a good man, am I?"

Amera turned to Curtis surprised by the question and the soft tone of his voice. They hadn't spoken since the child's rescue and she'd anticipated a silent drive back. "I'm sorry?"

"No one from the office came to see me in the hospital and at the factory I could tell they despise me."

"That's bound to happen when you value power more than respect."

He grinned. "I should have known you wouldn't contradict me."

"You'd know I was lying."

"And you don't lie to me?"

She hesitated. "I try my best not to."

"But sometimes you have no choice," he said watching her closely.

"Yes."

He nodded.

She cleared her throat. It was risky, but maybe she

could get to him in this sudden, reflective mood. "You were trying to change. Before your accident, you were going to reverse your decision about closing the factory."

"I was?"

"Yes."

Amera pulled out her tablet and showed him some data. "Not only is Valdan performing well, you'd scheduled to sign new contracts." She showed him a spreadsheet she'd worked on with Owen, of projected revenue expected if Curtis decided to deal with three major companies he'd been interested in partnering with. But he hadn't moved on the decision yet.

"Really?"

"Yes, not only will these contracts be lucrative, but they will help expand your markets without stretching you too thin and keep you in a field you dominate." She showed him an elaborate chart.

"*I* thought of this?"

"Of course. You're a brillant man."

"And my father agreed to this?"

"You went to key shareholders and convinced them first," Amera said prepared for the question. "Before approaching him."

"People don't usually make a move without my father's approval."

Amera bit her lip. He was right. "You came up with your strategy, but only told me. I'm sure an extension for Valdan, for a couple of months will give you time to remember," she said, desperate to make things work. At least for awhile.

"Be specific."

"Six months."

"Six is not 'a couple'."

"I meant a few." She bit her lip. "Maybe five."

"Three."

She nodded, trying not to appear overeager. "Yes, three that's what you said."

"I see."

Amera inwardly cheered. "Oh, and I forgot to show you something." She pulled out the bracelet Maya had given her. "This is for you."

"What is it?"

"It's from one of the girls at Peale House. You said you'd think about donating to them if she danced for you. Well, she did," Amera pulled up the video on her phone and played it, hoping the new rouse would work. She couldn't read his expression while he watched and felt her hope slipping.

"I can understand the dance," Curtis said when the video ended, "But why a bracelet?"

"She thought it would make you happy?"

He frowned. "Why would she think that?"

"It was the only way I could convince her to dance for you. I said a friend of mine--"

"A friend?"

"I couldn't very well tell her you were my bos-- husband. I didn't want to confuse her."

"Why would that confuse her?"

"I just didn't want her to know about our relation- ship, so I told her that my friend was sad but if she danced she might make him happy. So she did, then she also wanted to give you that," she said nodding to the bracelet.

Curtis ran his fingers over the beads and kept his gaze lowered. "Do you think I'm sad?"

"No."

"Then why did you tell her I was? Why didn't you just say your friend wanted to see her dance?"

"Because doing something for a purpose is sometimes easier than doing something just for show."

He lifted his gaze. "What do you mean?"

"Um...this probably won't make sense to you."

"Try me."

"Imagine being a baker."

He frowned. "I've never baked a thing in my life and-"

Amera shook her head. "Okay forget that. Don't imagine it. Let me tell you a story about two bakers."

He nodded. "Go on."

"The first baker only bakes for contests. His main concern is how he's perceived, how his product is thought of, and winning for himself. Being number one is the ultimate goal."

"Makes sense."

"The second baker only bakes for his neighbor. His neighbor is a shut in with no family, but every time he receives the baker's sweet cookies, he smiles and it makes him happy. And that makes the baker happy."

"What?"

"What do you mean?"

"What makes the baker happy?"

"Making the neighbor happy."

"But where's the real reward in that? At least the first baker is aiming for a goal and there's a measurable outcome. Either he wins or he loses. The second baker gets a smile, but what is a smile worth?"

"Exactly."

"Exactly what?"

"A smile is priceless."

Curtis shook his head. "This story doesn't make sense. I asked you why you didn't tell the little girl to just dance and you start talking about baked goods."

Amera sighed. "My point is that people don't always do something in order to get something tangible, like a prize or money or fame. Sometimes, it's easier to give something that helps someone else and the reward cannot be monetized or measured, but it's still valuable."

Curtis stared down at the bracelet and Amera knew that he still didn't understand fully. "Never mind," she said reaching for it.

He gripped it in his hand. "You said it's mine, right?"

"Yes."

"Then why are you trying to take it?"

"Because you'll probably throw it away."

"So? It's still mine."

"Give it to me."

He tucked it in his coat pocket. "No." He folded his arms. "She may not have given me this bracelet for a reward, but *you* did. How much do you want?"

She gave him a figure.

"Too much."

He was right, but she'd tried to give it a shot. "I have a proposal that you were considering. It has the specifics you like and anything that's confusing to you, I'll explain."

He rubbed the side of his head as if it hurt him. "Give me a minimum."

"A minimum?"

"Yes, say it quick."

She mentioned an amount then said, "Are you okay?" when he grimaced.

"I'm fine." He pulled out the bracelet. "The amount you just gave me is the cost of this. I'll write a check. You can give it to her later."

"I can't give a child that kind of money."

"Then I'll make it out to you."

"Or you can make it out to Peale House."

He pinched the bridge of his nose. "No, you can do that."

"Why don't you want to look at the propo--"

"Because my head hurts," he said resting his head against the back of the seat and closing his eyes.

"Do you want to take something?" Amera asked, suddenly concerned.

"No. It'll pass."

At least his nose wasn't bleeding, that was a good sign, but Amera put on classical music anyway to soothe him. The amount she'd asked for was much lower than the amount she'd asked for in her proposal, but at least now she could give Peale House something. Her heart sang. She couldn't believe her good fortune and she could hardly keep still the rest of the drive home. She felt like she was floating into the house when they finally arrived.

"I'm going to go change," Amera said, handing her coat to the maid. Having been to his place on numerous occasions, she was familiar with his house and knew where she'd be staying. However, when she passed by the living room she halted and did a double take. It looked nothing like she'd remembered. Curtis had a clean, austere decor, suitable for a bachelor. Now the living room looked as if it had been pulled out of an upscale magazine for home and hearth. A large decorated Christmas tree rested in the corner, two large crystal deer stood on either side of the fireplace where a lighted winter pine garland hung with a large wreath situated overhead. Silk Persian throw pillows sat on the couch, accented by silver gift boxes which lay on the side tables. Owen had outdone himself to make the place look like a home, she couldn't wait to see what he'd done to the guestroom.

"What are you looking at?" Curtis asked.

She gestured to the living room and watched him closely. "What do you think?"

"Should I think anything?"

Well, he wasn't put off by it, that was a good sign. That meant he accepted things as normal. "No." She turned to leave.

"Wait," Curtis said.

She turned to him, feeling her good mood waver. She

didn't like the serious tone of his voice. Had he changed his mind already? "What?"

"Who is Bill to you?"

"Bill? Bill Homer?"

Curtis folded his arms and nodded.

"He's one of the plant managers at--"

"I know who he is to the factory. I want to know who he is to you."

Amera started to smile. "You almost sound jealous."

"I am jealous," he said in a deep tone.

Her smile fell and she blinked, surprised by the ferocity of his gaze and the sincerity of his words. "It's nothing."

"Even when I was in the hospital, you didn't run to me that way. Are you seeing him?"

"He's a married man."

"That hasn't stopped people before."

She moved closer to him and took his arm. "Si-- Curtis, come and sit down."

He slipped out of her grasp and backed her against the wall, his arms on either side. "What have you done to me?"

She swallowed, as his gaze traveled over her face, her body responding to the nearness of him. She felt like asking him the same question. What had he done to her? Why was she responding to him this way? Why had his mouth suddenly become so fascinating to her? Why did the heat from his body seem to draw her closer? "I--"

"I'm not a jealous man," he cut in, his voice raw. "And usually I don't care what people think, but now..."

He briefly closed his eyes and shook his head. "Nothing makes sense."

Amera licked her lips, briefly wishing she could lick his lips too, before she berated herself. She had to stay sensible and in control. "It has been a very exhausting day. You need to rest."

He stood very still. "Who is Bill?"

She knew he wouldn't let it go. "He saved my life once, but he doesn't remember and you can't tell him."

"Why not?"

"Because it's none of your business."

"How can the man who saved my wife's life be none of my business?"

"Because I'm not--." She stopped before she told him the truth. It was too soon to stop the charade, especially when she'd made such great progress. "I'm not ready to tell him."

"Tell me when you are and I'll give him a reward."

"Really? What would you give him?" Amera asked, curious.

Curtis started to grin. "What do you have in mind?"

Amera folded her arms so that he wouldn't see her trembling hands. She didn't want him to see how important this was to her. "He has a son in college who's completing his master's and another son with special needs."

Curtis pushed himself from the wall and nodded. "Okay."

She stared at him confused. "Okay?"

"Consider it done." He turned to walk away.

She jumped in front of him, her heart pounding so fast she didn't feel she could catch her breath. "Consider what done?"

"You want his son's college debt to disappear and his other son's needs taken care of, correct?"

"Yes, but it has to be anonymous."

"Okay." He moved past her.

She jumped in front of him again. "Really?" she asked, unable to believe it. "You're not joking?"

"Why do you keep jumping in front of me like that? You know I don't joke."

Amera clasped her hands together, her heart bursting with delight. "You're really going to help Bill for me? You're really going to anonymously reward him for saving my life?"

"Yes."

She threw her arms around his neck and hugged him. "You don't know how much this means to me. All my life I've dreamt of this moment," she said, her voice shaking as tears of joy streamed down her cheeks. "Thank you, thank you so much."

"It's nothing," he said in a gruff tone.

Amera drew back and stared at him. "Maybe to you, but it's everything to me." She wiped her tears. "Let me go change."

"Did...did I make you happy?"

She turned to him surprised that he'd even need to ask. That he even cared. "Yes," she said then, spun around in a circle with her arms stretched wide as she'd seen Maya do, then blew him a kiss. "I'm over the moon."

He'd made her happy. And it had been so easy. So simple. Curtis walked into his bedroom with a smile. He wondered how he could come up with other ways to get her to hug him like that. He liked that feeling. It surprised him how much. No, it wasn't that much of a surprise anymore. He could no longer deny his attraction to her. And he realized he didn't want to. The feeling seemed to fuel him. It heightened his senses and made his mind a little sharper. He wanted to know more about her. How had Bill saved her life? Where did she go to school? What was her father like?

He sat on the side of his bed. What was even better was he sensed that she felt the attraction too. Or was she just playing along to get what she wanted? He'd been in enough relationships to know that he couldn't afford to be sentimental. She was probably only interested in his money and how much she could get out of him. So far she was batting a thousand, of course she'd be happy. Not because of him, but because of his money. The thought hurt, but he brushed it aside.

He had to remember this wasn't real. That the only reason he was continuing this charade was because he still needed to remember the details of that night. He still had a sense that he needed to protect her. But until his full memory returned, he couldn't let Amera have all the fun. His smile returned as an idea struck him, he planned to have some fun of his own.

Amera raced into the guestroom, closed the door then released a squeal of delight. She'd pulled it off! She couldn't believe her lie had really worked! He would keep the factory open a little longer *and* write a check to Peale House. But even better than that, he'd help Bill. This new Curtis was wonderful. Gruff, but generous. Curt, but compassionate. She wondered how long he thought they'd been married, she wouldn't dare ask him. She rested her hand over her still pounding heart. She was dangerously close to falling for him. But she couldn't. He wouldn't be like this forever. Once his memory returned all of this would fade away. The thought depressed her, but she decided not to focus on it. She'd enjoy what she could get from him now. She'd dreamed of revenge but it had looked nothing like this.

She opened the closet doors then stood paralyzed, stunned by the sight.

The walk-in closet was nearly the size of her apartment and looked like an exclusive boutique. Filled from top to bottom, it boasted an assortment of designer dresses, blouses, jackets, skirts, pants and several upscale suits. In addition, there were over thirty pairs of shoes, a wide variety of bags, and most of all, an elegant collection of fine jewelry. It was stunning. Unfortunately, none of it was hers.

CHAPTER 12

She pulled out her cell phone and called Owen. "You did a great job with the house, but where are my clothes?" she asked when he picked up.

"They haven't arrived yet?"

"No."

"You mean you have nothing to wear?" he said stunned.

"No, there are clothes here, but they aren't mine."

"That's strange. I took everything she gave me."

Amera paused. "She?"

"Yes, your maid."

"I don't have a maid."

"Oh, well, she was very convincing. Not as a maid, she didn't really look like a typical one, but she took total command of the move. She told me that she'd get in touch with you and explain everything."

"She hasn't and..." Amera paused when she saw a piece of paper with the word 'Scan' written across it. "I'll call you back." She disconnected with Owen then used her phone and scanned the paper. A video message popped up and an attractive dark, skinned woman appeared on the screen. The regal manner with which she held herself, immediately caught Amera's attention. Her thick hair was braided and pulled to one side held in place with several hand carved hair combs. Her stunning dark eyes were lined with a hint of purple eye shadow, and her lips looked like painted red wine.

"Welcome to your new wardrobe. I'm sure it was a surprise, but it's exactly what you need. No, don't ask how I know. That's not the point. Everything is in your size and yes, everything belongs to you--no returns. Your next task is to dress up and attend the office party."

Amera watched the video three more times, not believing it. All of this was hers? Really? She touched the silk and fine hand-woven fabric of one of the dresses. Then she pressed her cheek against a beautiful lingerie set and ran her hand through the collection of brightly colored lace underwear, neatly arranged in several rows in the scented drawers. She'd never gone to the office party before, but she definitely would now.

She turned on some holiday music, something she usually didn't do, but she felt as if Christmas had come early. Amera tried on several pairs of shoes and some of the jewelry with the enthusiasm of a little girl playing dress-up. Later, she grabbed several outfits and laid them out on the bed and tried them on. She was practicing some dance moves wearing one of the new dresses when she felt a presence. She spun around and saw Curtis staring at her from the doorway.

"I knocked," he said.

She turned off the music. "Oh, sorry, si-- Did you need something?"

"It takes you this long to change for dinner?"

She'd totally forgotten about dinner. "I'll be right there."

Curtis shrugged unconcerned then walked into the room, his gaze going over the selection of clothes lying on the bed and the open closet. "What are you doing?"

"Nothing," Amera said, starting to clean up. "How's your headache?"

"Gone. Looks like you're preparing for something."

She hung up a dress, there was no point in lying to him. "There's the office party."

He nodded. "Oh yes, I'd forgotten." He pointed to a purple dress. "Try that one on."

"What? Now?"

He nodded again.

"With you standing there?" she asked, nearly choking on her words.

He glanced at a chair. "You want me to sit down?"

"No, I mean. Why would you want to stay?"

He slowly closed the distance between them. "Is there anything wrong with a man watching his wife dress?" He lifted the dress off the bed.

Amera licked her lips. "No, but you usually don't."

He stood in front of her. "I've changed. Go on." He

handed her the dress. "Try this on first." He pointed to another. "Then I'd like to see you in that."

She swallowed. "Shouldn't we eat first?"

"We can eat later." He reached for her blouse. "Do you need me to help you?"

Amera stepped back, wishing he wouldn't stand so close, wishing his presence didn't make her body burn with longing. "No, I'll be fine. I'm sure it doesn't really matter what I wear."

"It matters to me."

She widened her eyes in fear. "You're not coming too," she said, more as a statement of fact than a question.

"You don't want me too?"

"It would be a disaster...I mean, you never go," she clarified. "You wouldn't enjoy it."

A mischievous grin spread on his face. "I know, plus nobody wants me there. I just wanted to see how you'd react. Now stop stalling. Every time you lick your lips like that, you make me want to kiss you."

She sucked her lips in and lowered her gaze. She wanted him to kiss her, she wanted him to do a lot more. But not now when the daylight could show all her imperfections. "This isn't like you."

He lifted her chin. "Look at me."

She reluctantly did.

"Are you really going to deny your husband this small pleasure?" he said his tone tinged with velvet persuasion.

"I told you that you don't like this."

"Refresh my memory."

There was no way she could win this argument. It

wasn't that she was being demur or shy but she never undressed in front of anyone because of one painful reason. She'd never expected to have to reveal it to him, especially now when what he thought mattered to her. She took a deep breath, maybe he'd never remember anyway, he certainly wouldn't ask her again after this. She took of her blouse then looked at him, gauging his reaction.

It was the look of defiance that heated his blood. He barely remembered the surprise he felt seeing the large scar that marred her chest, instead he remembered her eyes. Those light, compelling eyes mirroring a well of strength he'd always admired. He couldn't turn away from them, glad that they weren't filled with fear, but challenge. And that challenge aroused him. Never before had he seen how beautiful she was. Never before had he cared about the delicate shape of her nose, the smooth sheen of her skin, the fullness of her lips.

At first he'd wanted to get a little revenge for her deception about being his wife, and lying to him about the factory and Peale House. He didn't like how the bracelet and the image of the little girl dancing in the video shook him more than he wanted them too. And he hadn't lied about the headache, something bothered him about what Amera had been saying, but he couldn't grasp what. He hated her mentioning the proposal, but he couldn't figure out why. However, right now he didn't care about Peale House, the factory or revenge. All he cared about was how close Amera was to him and that it wasn't close enough. He pulled her into the circle of his arms and covered her mouth with his.

"I don't know what I'm doing," he whispered against her lips, but he couldn't stop himself, falling victim to his deep, primitive need. He hungrily reveled in the sweet taste of her mouth, moving quickly, fearful that she'd suddenly pull away. He groaned when he felt her arms circle his neck, pressing her body close to his, the pressure in his trousers building. He moved his mouth to the curve of her neck.

"This is why you don't watch me dress," she teased.

He laughed. "I'll try to remember next time." He pushed the clothes off the bed.

"We haven't eaten."

"So what?" he said, leading her over to the bed.

"But--"

"But what?" he asked taking off his shirt, but paused before taking off his trousers when he saw the look of hesitation on her face. He thought she felt the unexpected attraction as much as he did. Was he wrong? Had she kissed him back out of pity? Was sleeping with him going too far? He gritted his teeth, tapping down a feeling of anger and frustration. He wanted her, but he wouldn't force her. He had to get out because he if touched her again he wouldn't be able to stop himself. He zipped up his trousers and turned.

She grabbed his arm. "Wait."

He spun around. "If you've never been afraid of me

before, you should be afraid of me now," he said with a soft warning.

"We're not ready to have children yet."

"What?"

She cleared her throat. "I should know, but I don't know where you keep them."

"What the hell are you talking about? Be specific."

"You always use condoms."

He inwardly swore. She was right. He always did, he couldn't afford to make a mistake like that, he'd completely lost his mind. He'd never been with a woman without thinking of protection. Especially protection against a paternity suit, but for one wild moment that thought hadn't even entered his mind. And she could have taken advantage of him. If she'd had his child she would be set for life. At that moment, his respect for her solidified into complete admiration. "You're right," he said going over to the side table. He always kept condoms there in the guestroom. He never let ladies into his master bedroom. "I may have forgotten that, but at least I remembered that I always keep them here because you hate being in my room."

"Oh right," Amera said clearly relieved that he'd overlooked her ignorance. She lowered her gaze and unzipped her skirt.

Curtis suppressed a smile. "Anything else I should remember?"

"Um, I don't think so," she said pulling off her stockings.

For a second Curtis imagined her wearing a crotchless pair, and thought of how much fun that would be. He shook his head, snapping himself out of the fantasy, he'd think of that another time. He lowered his body over hers, and explored her thighs and her breasts, fondling her nipples with his hands and then his tongue. He had to time it right, he couldn't move too fast because he didn't want to scare her, but he couldn't move too slowly because that would kill him. He entered her with deliberate mastery, but the moment still shocked them both. She gasped, he groaned then squeezed his eyes shut and swore.

Could he be her first? Why would she wait for someone like him? No, maybe he wasn't. Some woman stayed tight. Damn, he couldn't even ask her. But the moment he looked into her eyes he knew. She'd never been with another man and she'd chosen him. This wasn't an accident, but a decision. He felt as if something inside him had splintered and shattered. As if a glass wall that had separated him from everyone else had been broken, magnifying his feelings, making him crave her touch even more. Increasing his desire to please her.

At first he moved gingerly and with care, knowing there were no words he could say to her to help them both save face. Her movements were awkward at first, then she began to relax and follow his lead. He used his body to speak and she responded, arching her body into his, her legs wrapping around him, drawing him in deeper.

He hadn't planned on this being part of the deception. Everything he felt was real, alarmingly so. He'd never known the strength of such emotion and he didn't know how to detain it, or keep it at bay. With every touch and caress, he surrendered, his inner battle growing more intense as his passion grew. *I will keep you safe*, he silently vowed. He would unlock the mystery of his mind and figure out what the danger was.

Curtis gazed down at his wife, for at that moment he decided that's what she would be, and he saw his equal. *Marry me*, he wanted to say, but couldn't. There were still too many questions. What if she didn't want to bond with him for life? Unlike Crystal, he couldn't face that rejection and that made him feel ashamed because a Bishop didn't care. He was never supposed to care.

He glanced down and saw a red drop fall on her chest. He sniffed then rubbed his nose, he looked at the blood on his hand and swore.

"What's wrong?" Amera asked.

He sat up with self-loathing. "Nothing."

She grabbed his arm, with surprising strength, before he could turn away, and in a very low, calm voice said, "It's okay. Stay still." However, it wasn't the same calm voice she usually used with him after an episode. It wasn't cold and dismissive. There was a deeper, more tender undertone or did he just imagine it that way? She handed him some tissues, then wiped her chest. "Don't worry. It's happened before."

She was lying to him and she looked at him without judgment, igniting a pain in his heart that gripped him then disappeared. Did that mean she truly cared about him too? That with time he could persuade her to stay with him? To make this farce a reality? For the first time Curtis didn't care how pathetic his hope made him seem or what his father would say. He was alone with her and would savor the moment.

"It's stopped now." She threw her tissue away. "But you should rest."

He didn't want her to see him as weak. He wanted to tell her that it wouldn't happen again because he wasn't ashamed of his feelings. But he didn't have the words. He didn't know the language of emotion. How to express himself that way. So he decided to change the subject. He gently ran his hand over her scar. "What's this?" he asked, then remembered he should know the answer. "I mean I've never asked how you got this scar."

"It's one of the reasons I was never adopted."

"You were an orphan? I know I should remember but my mind is still fuzzy." All these years and he knew so little about her.

She nodded. "I grew up in an orphanage." She told him about her life growing up in two orphanages and shared that as a child, she had had an unfortunate accident, when she and another child were playing with a ball, and she ran into one of the kitchen staff and hot oil got spilled on her chest.

"How did Bill save your life?"

"There was a clinic run by Doctors Without Borders where I was taken. The wound became infected. I don't remember much, but I do remember he was the doctor who treated me. He was so kind to me during my hospital stay and even visited me at the orphanage." She looked away and for a moment he thought he saw the glistening of tears but when she looked at him again, they were gone. "I always wanted to be adopted. First I wasn't cute enough and then I was too old. Fortunately, I was bright."

"What happened to your parents?"

"Both dead. I don't know how. Don't care how because it wouldn't change anything."

Curtis silently swore. She was an orphan with no ties. That would be a problem. His father liked to know a person's bloodlines, but he'd handle that problem when the time came. He gathered her close, as if protecting her from that threat. He'd deal with everything one at a time. First, he had to remember the reflection in the car mirror and why her umbrella mattered.

"You're still tense," she said, her head resting on his chest.

"There's something I'm trying to remember," he said, he didn't want her worrying about another nosebleed. But when he felt her stiffen, he realized he'd said the wrong thing. If she knew he got his memory back, it meant the end of their charade. Ending it now wasn't an option, not until his memory was whole again. "I think I saw who attacked me," he clarified. He felt her relax.

"Your memory will soon come back to you." She lifted her head and looked at him. "I know this might not be the right time to say this, but--"

He kissed her. He didn't want to hear what she had to say. He didn't want to talk anymore. As he held her in his arms he was free from doubt, from worry, from shame and when they became one again, all he wanted to do was delve into sweet ecstasy.

She was an evil woman. Amera lifted herself up on her side of the bed and gazed down at Curtis as he lay sleeping on his back. She didn't know how he could stay so still. He was a marvelous, wonderful, magnificent lover. She'd never had sex before and now she wanted to do it again and again and again with no one but him. He exceeded her every imagination. Not that she imagined a lot. She'd heard women discuss sex, some with disdain and some with awe, but she'd always thought it would be something nice to try sometime.

But it was better than 'nice' it was even better than 'good'. She couldn't come up with enough superlatives that satisfied her. He'd awakened a woman in her she hadn't even known had been asleep. All her senses felt alive--colors seemed brighter, sounds clearer, the scent of his skin like an intoxicating aroma. He was amazing and she was taking advantage of him. It was one thing to change his mind about closing the factory and getting money for Peale House, and even getting him to help Bill, but to use his body for her own pleasure? She had crossed the line.

Why did he have to be so good at it? Why did it have to feel so right? She'd felt certain her deception had been discovered when his nose started to bleed. For a moment, she expected him to come to his senses and say 'What the hell am I doing?' but instead he looked embarrassed. He'd never been embarrassed about his nosebleeds before, not with her. And, as she grabbed the tissues, she felt as if this was where she belonged. By his side. Not just in bed, but always.

"How long are you going to stare at me like that?" Curtis asked, his eyes still closed.

Amera sighed. She should forget about the office party and the clothes, pretending to be his wife and getting revenge. Sure, she could use him, but she was hurting herself. The awful thing was that she liked him now. Much more than she should.

Curtis opened his eyes. "What's wrong?"

Amera bit her lip then said, "I'm an evil woman."

His face relaxed into a wicked grin. "And I'm a bad man."

She shook her head. "It's not the same."

He stood up and started to change. "Let's eat," he said pulling up his pants. He turned to her and winked, making her heart leap. "Then you'll model what you plan to wear to the office party."

"What's this?" Florence asked looking at the check Amera had handed her.

"It's exactly what it looks like."

"A check made out to you."

"I signed it over to Peale House on the back. Happy holidays."

"How did you get him to do this?"

She didn't want to tell her friend about her deception. Only she and Owen could know about it. "He owed me a favor."

Amera was glad to be out of the house away from him, although distance didn't keep him far from her mind. They'd spent most of the last two days in bed and when they weren't in bed they hotly debated topics they'd never agree on, and discussed some projects he wanted to launch in the future. She liked his sharp mind, how he challenged her and treated her as his equal. Their topics of conversation weren't sexy, but they were real. She got to see another side to him--a human side. That morning she'd seen how much so. She had been sneaking a melon from the fruit spread the chef had laid out when she heard Curtis' footsteps.

She turned around and screamed.

CHAPTER 13

Curtis spun around then stared back at her confused when he didn't see anything behind him. "What?"

He was a shark in a suit. He looked so much like the old Curtis that Amera half expected him to demand what she was doing in his house. Could his memory have returned already? Amera leaned against the kitchen island unable to get her mouth to move. She hadn't seen him in a suit since he'd left the hospital.

Curtis took a hesitant step forward. "Are you okay?"

No, his memory hadn't returned. He wouldn't have asked her that if it had. She started to relax, then felt foolish for her outburst. "Yes, I'm sorry." Amera cleared her throat. "I didn't hear you coming." She sat down and took a deep, shaky breath.

He sat down beside her. "Are you sure you're okay?"

"Yes," she said, looking out at the clear December morning and the manicured lawn. She couldn't look at him, not yet. "Why are you dressed up?" she asked, trying to sound casual.

"Because I'm going out."

Amera turned to him alarmed. "You can't."

"Why not?"

"Because you still need to rest."

Curtis rested his arm on the back of her chair and leaned in to kiss her on the neck. "Thanks to you, I feel very rested."

The warm pressure of his lips made her skin tingled. She touched a hand to her face, feeling flustered. That was a problem. She couldn't be flustered, she had to always be two steps ahead of him. If she'd been thinking correctly, over the weekend she would have been prepared for Monday and a moment like this. She hadn't even thought about how she could get her job back. Her two weeks were up. How could she tell him that he'd fired her, but had made a mistake? Plus, she couldn't have anyone at the office know about them being married.

"I still think you should take another week. At least until after Christmas."

Curtis leaned back in his chair. "Do I look like my father to you?"

"Yes."

His eyes slightly narrowed. "I meant, do I look like the kind of man who needs to work from home because he's so sick?"

"Oh," Amera said, clearing her throat and feeling her face grow warm.

"I'm not my father."

"I didn't say you were," she said surprised by the ice in his tone. "Just that you look like him. Except..." She let her words fall away.

"Except what?"

"You're better looking."

Curtis rubbed his chin clearly pleased by her words. "Of course."

"Now about work--"

"I'm not going to the office. I have other errands I want to do, so you have the day off." He stood up then bent down to kiss her. "I'll see you at dinner."

"But--"

"Don't worry," he said heading down the hall. "I won't over do it."

Amera jumped up and followed him. "You haven't eaten breakfast."

He put on his jacket. "I'll grab something later."

"But where are you going?"

He grinned. "If you must know, I haven't done my holiday shopping yet." He kissed her again then left.

Holiday shopping. She hadn't expected him to say that. He was just one surprise after another. But the sight of him in a suit had shaken her and persuaded her to give Florence the check he'd written out to her, before his memory returned. She wasn't fully sure how to deal with a man who looked like Curtis, but didn't always act like him. Should she buy him something for Christmas? It was next week. Should she stay around that long? How could she convince him to stay home the rest of the week?

These thoughts filled her mind after she left Florence

and wandered the shopping mall. She didn't know what to get him. He was a man who had everything--except a real wife.

"What did she come by for?" Vernon asked, looking through the window to watch Amera get in her car.

"She came to drop off a check."

He turned to her. "Don't cash it."

Florence waved the check. "Why not? Money is money." She held the check with both hands and held it like a banner. "And look at all those pretty zeros."

"I don't have a good feeling about it."

"What's wrong with you?" Florence put the check in a drawer then locked it. "You've been real jumpy these last few days."

He returned his gaze to the window. "I've just got a few things on my mind."

Florence came from behind the desk, stood beside him and said in a soft voice, "What things?"

Damn, he wished he could tell her, but he knew he couldn't. "You know I don't like her coming here. What if you cash that check and she starts asking how we spent it?"

"I'll give her a good story." She wrapped her arms around his waist and rested her head against his back. "Relax, it's not that much and it should keep her at bay for awhile. I don't think we have anything to worry about."

Vernon held her close, hoping she was right.

Bill rubbed his eyes in disbelief when he saw Curtis enter the factory. He rushed up to him, ready to report. "Sir, as you can see, everything is running on schedule. The machine wasn't damaged as a result of the accident and we only lost a few hours that day so--"

"Where's the mother?"

"She's over there," he said, pointing to one of the machines. "She's very sorry about--"

"Bring her and her brother to see me," he said turning towards the office.

"May I ask where Ms. Thurston is?"

"No."

Bill silently swore. At least Amera could give him a clue as to what Curtis was thinking. He reluctantly gathered Maria and her brother Jorge and told them to follow him. They were excellent workers. Their family was third generation Pennsylvanians, who'd fallen on hard times, and he hated knowing that soon they'd have to look elsewhere for employment.

"Sit down," Curtis said once they entered the office.

The two sat, their eyes never leaving him. Bill stood off to the side.

Curtis held his hands behind his back. "How is your son?"

"Fine," Maria said in a shaky voice. "He'll be able to keep his hand."

"Good."

"But--," she stopped when her brother sent her a hard look.

"But what?" Curtis said.

"Nothing sir," Jorge said.

He looked at Maria. "Is that true?"

"Yes," she said in a small voice.

"Okay." He nodded at Jorge. "That's a quality shirt you're wearing. I noticed you wearing a similar one the other day. Where did you get them?"

"My sister made them."

"Really? You have your own business?"

"No, sir," she said quickly. "It's just something I do on the side."

He nodded. "Make me three shirts and I'll pay for your son's extra medical expenses."

She gasped and tears sprung to her eyes. She surged to her feet and clasped her hands together. "Oh sir, thank you."

Curtis turned to Bill embarrassed by her exuberance. "Get a tape measure."

"Sir, we can't thank you enough," Jorge said, shaking his hand.

"It's a simple exchange," Curtis said in gruff tone. "One that no one can know about."

Making people happy was so easy, Curtis thought on his drive home. He hadn't gone there initially to do so, but he didn't regret it. Out of habit, he turned to ask Amera her opinion then remembered that she wasn't there and he couldn't let her know what he was up to. It had been an exploratory visit because he'd noticed the young man's shirt and wanted to know who made it. When it came to clothing, he could always spot fine craftsmanship. Bill was right, Valdan had a talented work force. While Maria took his measurements, he'd learned that Jorge had gotten a computer degree, but worked at the factory because he'd learned some outdated computer languages and hadn't been able to get a job in the field. He could get the factory to stay open a little longer, but perhaps there was a way to keep it open permanently.

Feeling sorry for the rats? Do you want to be a rat too? Curtis winced as if his father had spoken the words and followed them with a slap. It didn't matter, if no one knew about it. He couldn't be seen as weak. But it felt strange that seeing Maria and Jorge's joy made him feel strong not weak. It didn't make sense. Why would his father and grandfather warn him against this? He must be missing something. He rubbed the side of his head feeling a headache begin to develop. He had to tread carefully.

He took out his cell phone to make a dinner reservation and started to dial then stopped. He couldn't take Amera out. They couldn't be seen together as a couple if he wanted this charade to work. He put his phone away. Fortunately, it didn't stop him from shopping for a gift.

Two hours later he regretted the impulse. He sat in a luxury department store with two personal shoppers on either side of him and a host of items displayed in front of him with no clue what to choose. He'd never had to shop for someone before. He'd always had someone else do that trivial act for him. And for the past five years that person had been Amera. He now realized how little he knew about her. He knew her past and that Bill had saved her life, but he didn't know what colors she liked or if she'd prefer hand beaded crystal jewelry over an Australian glass vase.

He stood hating the feeling of inadequacy. "Never mind."

"Sir," one of the attendants said. "If you'd like--"

"I'm fine," he said heading for the door.

"Curtis?"

He paused then briefly closed his eyes. He knew that voice and she was the last person he wanted to see right now. She had no right to call his name. He took a deep breath then slowly spun around. "Crystal."

She took a quick step back, as if she'd just approached a dangerous animal. "I'm sorry."

He took a step forward. "Why?"

Her voice rose a notch and she took another step back. "I heard about your attack. I'm glad you're alright."

Curtis stopped. Scaring her was fun, but it wasn't fair. She was too easy a target. "Thank you."

She gave a nervous laugh. "Never thought I'd find you in a place like this. Are you getting something for Amera?"

He stilled, trying to process he words. "What?"

Her hand flew to her mouth. "Oh, I forgot I wasn't

supposed to say anything."

"Amera told you about us?"

Crystal shook her head. "No, I figured it out when I saw the ring."

"Before or after my accident?"

She shook her head again, this time with agitation. "I--I don't remember."

"Try."

"I think it was before."

"Do you think or do you know?"

"I don't..wait." Crystal pulled out her phone. "I had an appointment that day I can check. Yes, yes it was definitely before." She looked up at him curious. "Does it make a difference?"

Yes, he thought feeling the tension in him relax. Owen hadn't lied to him when he said only he and Amera knew about his memory loss. Amera hadn't bragged to others about being his wife. That was good. "Do you like Amera?"

"Yes."

He pointed at her. "Then don't make a slip like that again, to anyone. Not even her."

"Okay. Do you need some help?"

"Help?"

"Were you planning on getting something for her? I can't think of another reason why you'd be shopping in the women's department."

She was right and he wasn't too proud to get help. "What would you suggest giving a woman going to a party?"

CHAPTER 14

She was living a fairy tale, Amera thought as she made her way around the elegant ballroom beaming with holiday lights and decorations. She wore a blue lace bodice gown and Curtis had given her a stunning Tahitian pearl necklace and had her driven to the event. He made her feel like a princess, but the moment she entered the room she felt like a queen. All eyes turned to her. She'd never had that happen before. She was used to that happening when she was at Curtis' side, never by herself. Women looked at her with envy, men looked with lascivious interest. They asked her to dance, held out her chair and chatted with her.

"Excuse me," Owen said, expertly pulling her into a dancer's pose and away from her latest male companion. "Where's Bishop?"

"He's at home."

"I'm surprised he let you leave the house. You're a vision."

"Thank you."

"Are you sure he's not hiding somewhere ready to come out and grab me for dancing with his wife?"

Amera laughed, amused by the idea. "I'm positive. He'd never come to one of these events."

"Even for you?"

"I told him not to come."

"And I bet you regret that."

The truth of his words surprised her. Yes, she missed him. She wished she could have had a chance to dance with him. But he didn't like to dance. Except for Monday, he'd spent the rest of the week working from home and she'd grown accustomed to his presence. She'd given up the idea of trying to get her job back, because once his memory returned she planned to be as far away from him as possible. "No, he wouldn't have enjoyed himself and neither would anyone else."

"True. So how are things going so far?"

"Great I'm making real progress. He's looking into keeping the factory open."

Owen's brows shot up. "Wow, love really does change a person."

"Love?"

"You know what I mean."

"No, I don't. Be specific."

He grinned. "You're starting to sound like your husband."

Amera stopped dancing. "Do you think his memory loss is amusing?"

"No. I just--."

"I already feel guilty as it is. I've considered ending it tomorrow."

"No, don't do that," Owen said quickly.

"Why not?"

"Because you're doing so much good. Bishop had me look some more into Valdan."

"Good? Is it really good to use someone like this? He's not himself. Even you think his behavior is out of character. He thinks--"

"He's in love with you," Owen finished.

"He hasn't said that."

"Does he have to?"

"But it's not real." Amera looked down at her dress then around at the festivities. "None of this is real."

Owen began to reply when his cell phone rang. He looked at the number and swore. "I have to take this, but don't go anywhere," he said then left.

He wasn't supposed to envy the cockroaches. He wasn't supposed to want to be a rat, even for a minute. But he did. Curtis watched from the balcony as Amera made her way around the ballroom floor below. The week had gone by too fast and he was running out of time. He had to remember what was important about that night before his charade unraveled. He'd gone back to the parking lot twice, retracing his steps, but still nothing came to him.

He sighed and rested his hands on the railing. He'd never attended the office party before, but tonight he couldn't stay away. He wanted to be where she was. For just one night, he wanted to be an ordinary man. He didn't want to be separated from everyone. For the first time in his life, being a winner felt lonely. He wished he could dance with Amera as the other men did. He had to stop himself from going down and claiming her. When he saw Owen take her to the middle of the dance floor some of his tension ebbed, but not by much. He saw the two of them talking and wondered what they were saying. He pulled out his cell phone and sent Owen a text.

Minutes later Owen came running up to him. "What's wrong? I didn't know you were here. Why are you hiding? Why aren't you with her?"

Curtis gripped the railing and kept his voice low. "Are you being dumb on purpose or are you trying to make me laugh?"

"It's just that she misses you."

Curtis looked at him sharply. "Did she say that?"

"No, but I could tell."

"How?"

Owen rubbed the back of his neck, confused. "What do you mean 'how'?"

"How would you know if she didn't tell you?"

Owen shrugged. "You just get a sense."

"A sense of what?" Curtis snapped.

"You really can't be this clueless about your wife."

Curtis' gaze darkened. "She's *not* my wife and you know that."

"Right," Owen said sounding unconvinced. "And you

don't love her and she doesn't love you and this is all one big charade."

"Exactly."

Owen ran a tired hand down his face. "You two could drive me to drink." He shoved his hands in his pockets and shook his head. "Wait, you already did that. Never mind."

Curtis frowned. "Are you drunk right now?"

"No, but this conversation makes me regret not being so." He held up his hands in surrender. "Fine, I'll do what you want. You want to keep this charade going?"

"I don't have a choice," Curtis said in a grim tone.

Owen sighed. "Okay. But what about her?"

His tone hardened. "What about her?"

"She's thinking of telling you the truth."

Curtis felt his heart pick up pace. Didn't she like pretending to be his wife? Did dancing with all the men change her opinion of him? He was certain the bond they felt was mutual and DeWall had said she missed him. But DeWall hadn't given him specifics, just a feeling. Could he trust feelings? Maybe not, but he wasn't ready to lose her yet. "What did you say?"

"I tried to convince her not to."

"'Tried' is not an outcome. Did you succeed or not?"

Owen shrugged. "I don't know. I was talking to her when you called."

"Convince her to give me more time. Another week."

Owen gave a low whistle. "That's stretching it. You think you'll get your full memory back by then?"

No, but he needed more time to convince her that he was the man for her. "Yes."

Owen nodded. "Then I'll make it happen."

"Is something the matter?" Amera asked concerned when Owen returned with a frown.

"You're having a good time. I don't want to worry you."

"About what?"

"I just got a call from Bishop and some of the things he said didn't make sense. I was just reminded of how his doctor said that shock could be detrimental. I understand that this is hard for you, but C-couldn't you just keep this up for another week?"

Amera bit her lip, part of her eager to keep the charade going, but part of her knowing the longer they kept it up, the greater the risk of discovery. "You said a few days. We've already--"

"This is really something you two should talk about," he mumbled.

"What?"

He shook his head. "Nothing. Just that I think it's for the best. Just keep it going for a few more days. Maybe you could take him away somewhere."

Amera tilted her head, thoughtful. "His brother invited him for the holidays. There are five days to Christmas so there's still enough time."

Owen stiffened with alarm. "Uh, that's not what I was--"

Amera clapped her hands together, warming to the idea. "This would be great."

"How about something a little more romantic?"

"A family reunion for the holidays. I can just picture it now. His mother really wants to see him. This may be her last chance."

"I don't think--."

"Now I won't feel so guilty because I'll be doing something for him. He should be with his family for the holidays. Please help me make that happen."

"But--."

Amera smiled pleased with her plan. "I don't expect you to do much, just explain the situation to them. I'll make this a holiday to remember."

CHAPTER 15

Someone was going to pay for this. Curtis sat beside Amera in a quiet rage as she drove up to his brother's house. A place he'd never visited but only knew from a picture his brother had once shown him. He hadn't even known her intention until that moment. He'd trusted her. He'd willingly let her take him here. She said she had a special surprise for him. She'd turned him into a fool.

"What is this?" he asked when she parked.

"We decided to visit your family this year."

Curtis bit inside his cheek. She'd turned him into a sucker. He still remembered the night they had together after she returned from the holiday party and the three days after it--he'd flown her to London for a shopping spree. He hadn't been on guard when he should have.

Yes, someone had to pay. He didn't know when. He didn't know how, he didn't even know who--whether it should be Owen for not warning him or Amera. He didn't mind her deception about the factory, but coming up with a family gathering was something else. He could end things now. He could tell her that his memory was back and that he knew they weren't really married. Then he wouldn't have to see his mother again and pretend that things were okay. But he couldn't. Not until that one key memory came back.

He'd tried to hypnotize himself to remember, meditated, tried to get into a dream state but nothing worked.

"I've changed my mind."

"It's just for two days."

"I don't care," he said, wondering how he could fight her without revealing the truth. He gripped his hands into fists. "Let's go. Now."

"But your brother's already seen us."

"I don't care. Do you want me to drive?"

She gripped his hands. "Please give this a chance. We've worked hard on this visit."

Dammit, why did she sound so sincere? What was she getting out of this? He silently swore again and got out of the car.

"Hey Amera, Curtis, glad you could make it," Kyle said giving him a friendly, hearty pat on the back. "Your room is at the top of the stairs second to the left."

Curtis took their bags and headed in that direction.

"If you need a hand--"

"I'm fine," Curtis said, pushing past him. Behind him he heard his brother say, "Are you sure this is good idea? He doesn't look too happy to be here."

"At least your mother will get to see him," Amera said.

"She should be here soon, she went to get her hair done. She wanted to look her best."

Curtis stormed into the house, found the guest bedroom where they would stay, then threw the suitcases on the bed. Dammit, she'd gotten his brother in on it too. Of course. That was the only way it would work. Would he ask for another donation to his charity? What would his mother want? He was just one big checkbook to them. Curtis glanced at his watch. He'd only been there ten minutes and he hated it. How could he stomach two days? He sat down on the bed and swore. Come on...why couldn't he remember?

"Are you okay?"

He glanced up and saw Amera. He still couldn't figure out how she benefited from all this. "I'm fine."

"Do you have a headache?"

"All the time."

"Let me--"

He leaned against the headboard and stretched out his legs. "I'm fine."

"Your brother's about to give me a tour of the house. Want to join us?"

He closed his eyes. "No."

"Okay," she said, then he heard her leave.

He'd never been to his brother's house before and this would be the last time so it didn't matter if he saw it or not. He sat on the bed for a few minutes then grew restless and left the room. He found the living room, grabbed a remote and sat down. Before he could turn on the TV, a woman walked into the room then halted. She looked at him and gasped, covering the slight curve of her belly, as if she expected him to attack her. Her fear didn't surprise or annoy him. He was used to it. "You weren't expecting me?"

"No," Heidi said. "I mean, I thought Kyle was showing you the house."

"He's showing Amera."

"Yes." She pulled on the hem of her shirt. "Would you like something to drink?"

Before Curtis could decline they heard a thud upstairs then a loud wail. Heidi turned and ran. Curtis followed her. She ran into one of the rooms where he saw a little boy and an overturned crib. The little boy had evidently tried to climb out of it and had fallen over.

"Oh my dear, are you okay? Mommy's here." She picked up the child and hugged him while Curtis watched. Kyle and Amera came running into the room.

"What happened?" Kyle demanded.

"He tried to crawl into the crib again."

"Son, you get the big boy bed now."

The boy's tears continued to flow.

"But you don't want that do you?" Curtis said. He understood the boy's anger and tears, having felt them himself. "You don't want the big bed and you don't want to be the big brother. You want to be the baby again. I know. I didn't want to be a big brother either." He looked around the room then started to leave.

"Why?" a little voice asked.

Curtis slowly turned. "It's a secret."

The little boy wiped his eyes. "I'm good with secrets."

"Secrets only big brothers can know."

The boy looked at him and his eyes again filled with tears and his mouth moved but Curtis knew he was too young to have the words to share how he felt. "Come on. I'll tell you outside."

The boy grabbed onto his hand. Curtis felt awkward holding something so small, so trusting, but decided not to think about it. The boy needed space and so did he. "I'll be right back."

"Do you think we should follow them?" Heidi said.

"He's not going to hurt a child," Amera said.

"At least he got him to stop crying," Kyle said.

"He took him outside," Heidi said looking at them through the window. The two sat on the swing set.

Kyle joined her. "I wonder what he's saying I've never seen Damon so still."

"He probably likes the attention," Amera said.

Heidi shivered. "You'd think he'd be afraid of him. I am."

Amera nodded. "Most people are."

"I should go down. It's too cold for Damon to be out long."

"It's not that cold," Kyle said.

"You think I can't take care of my son?"

Kyle sighed. "No, but you do know how to ruin a good thing."

"What's that supposed to mean?"

Amera looked at the couple feeling the tension in the air. "If you're really uncomfortable I'll go--"

"He's fine," Kyle said returning his gaze to the window.

Heidi headed for the door. "I'm going to--"

Kyle's mouth fell open. "Oh my God."

She spun around and rushed over to the window. "What?"

"He's laughing. Curtis got him laughing."

Amera looked and saw Damon doubled over in laughter. He looked up at Curtis with a big grin then fell on the floor and laughed again. "I wonder what he's saying to him."

"Whatever it is, it's working," Kyle said. "I can't believe it."

"I didn't know your brother was funny," Heidi said.

"He's not," Kyle and Amera said in unison.

"But this reminds me of something," Kyle said in an odd tone.

"What?" Amera asked.

He shook his head. "I'm not sure."

They saw Curtis stand and Damon raced up to him and grabbed his hand again. Curtis playfully pushed him away. He grinned and grabbed his arm. Curtis looked down at him and said something that had the boy in giggles again. When the pair rejoined them Damon announced,

"I'm going to be the best big brother in the world. Right Uncle Curtis?"

He nodded.

Damon giggled.

"What did you talk about?" Amera asked.

Curtis playfully patted her cheek. "It's a secret."

"I like secrets."

He winked. "I know."

Heidi took her son's hand. "Come on, it's time to start cooking dinner. Kyle, set the table."

"I will in a minute," he said.

She shot him a look. "I need you to do it now."

He sighed then left.

Amera turned to Curtis. "I didn't know you were so good with kids."

"I'm not," Curtis said, glancing around the room. "Can we go now?"

"We just got here."

"I think we should leave before things get complicated."

"What could be complicated about being with your family?"

He shook his head and opened his mouth to reply when the sound of shattering glass pierced the air followed by raised voices.

Curtis rubbed the back of his neck. "Now, *this* is the kind of family holiday I remember."

Amera raced downstairs with Curtis behind her.

"I wasn't the one who wanted a second baby," she overhead Kyle say.

"So, now this is my fault?" Heidi shouted.

"Let me help you," Amera said coming into the kitchen and taking the broom and duster from Heidi. Damon sat quiet in the corner tightly holding a toy.

"Sorry," Heidi said. "We didn't mean to disturb you."

"It's okay," Amera said.

Kyle left the room.

When Curtis didn't move, Amera nudged him.

"What?" he asked.

"Go," she said in a low voice.

"Where?"

"Find out what's wrong."

Curtis pointed to the floor. "That's why I'm here."

She nudged him again. "Find out what's wrong with your brother. He probably wants to talk."

"What if I don't want to talk?"

She nudged him a third time. "Then just listen."

Curtis folded his arms and kept his feet planted. "I don't like doing that either."

"It's okay," Heidi said before Amera could argue. "He doesn't have to. I don't want you two involved with our problems." She sniffed.

Amera sent Curtis a stern look.

He blinked, looking bored.

She pulled him over to the side and whispered in his ear. "Please do this. Heidi looks really upset."

"If I do what you ask, can we leave?"

"Your mother hasn't seen you yet."

"That's not what I asked."

"Okay," Amera said reluctantly. She could understand his unease. This wasn't the holiday gathering she'd had in mind. She felt woefully ill-equipped to handle it-- she'd take a business deal collapse over family drama any day.

"Promise?"

"Yes."

"Good. Be careful," he said before he left.

Amera didn't understand the need for a warning, but was relieved that he hadn't argued. She led Damon to the family room and turned on a cartoon then returned to Heidi who was standing by the kitchen sink. "Why don't you sit down?" she suggested as she cleared up the glass.

Heidi covered her face with her hands. "I'm so ashamed."

"There's nothing to be ashamed of, accidents happen and couples fight."

"I didn't expect it to be this way, but seeing you with Curtis makes me see how horrible my marriage is."

"Kyle loves you and--"

Her hands fell to the table and she looked at Amera with red rimmed eyes. "Not as much as Curtis loves you."

"Curtis doesn't love me," Amera said with a laugh, amused by the statement. Both Kyle and Heidi knew about Curtis' memory loss and Amera's deception. She lowered her voice. "Remember, our marriage isn't real and--"

Heidi shook her head. "You don't see the way he looks at you."

Amera sat down at the kitchen table and took Heidi's hand in pity. Perhaps this was why Curtis had warned her to be careful. Because Heidi was pregnant, her hormones were clearly all over the place and confusing her. She had to be gentle with her. "First, the man out there is not the real Curtis. Second, it's easy to perceive what isn't there."

Heidi frowned. "What?"

Amera scratched her cheek, knowing she wasn't making herself clear. "You're imaging what you want to see. Even though you know my marriage is fake, you're imaging what it could be. What your marriage could be."

"The women aren't my imagination."

Amera released her hand and sat back in her chair, trying to process Heidi's words. "I'm sorry?"

"Kyle's cheated on me."

"Are you sure? Maybe--"

Heidi sniffed and wiped away a tear. "He doesn't even try to hide it anymore."

Amera wished she knew what to say, but didn't. Now all she wanted was to go home as much as Curtis did. Kyle cheated on his wife? He seemed so amiable and loyal. But why would she lie about that? Amera felt completely out of her depths. She was used to facts and figures. Affairs of the heart frightened her. "So you're divorcing him?"

"No," Heidi said stunned. She looked at Amera horrified. "I love him."

"Has he threatened to leave you?"

"No."

"Then what's the problem?" Amera asked confused.

Heidi wiped her eyes with a napkin and said with a reluctant smile. "You'd make a terrible counselor."

"I know. I'm not good at this. Let me help you with dinner," Amera said going to the fridge, hoping Curtis was having better luck with his brother. Fifteen minutes later she received a text on her cell phone from Curtis asking her to meet him in their bedroom. When she entered their room she saw him opening the closet.

"We're leaving now before it gets really ugly," Curtis said grabbing their suitcases. He shook them. "Why are these empty?"

"I unpacked them after Kyle gave me the house tour."

"I forgot how efficient you are," he grumbled opening a drawer.

"Did you know he's cheating on her?"

Curtis placed his clothes in the suitcase. "And the second child isn't his."

Her mouth dropped open. "How do you know?"

"He had a vasectomy."

"Without her knowledge? Isn't that illegal?"

Curtis looked up at her and grinned. "What are you going to do? Arrest him?"

Amera placed her hands on the side of her face and held her head. "What a mess. I didn't expect--"

"A dysfunctional family? Growing up you filled your mind with children's books and expected sing-alongs by the fire, lots of presents around the Christmas tree and laughter, right?"

"I'm sorry." She'd never considered that there may

have been other reasons why he hadn't wanted to visit his family all these years.

"Why? You're not responsible for what's happening. You didn't make them that way." He looked at her. "Why aren't you packing?"

"I'm sorry because I lied. You didn't want to come here."

"I know." He lifted a sly brow when she looked at him shocked. "I've lost my memory, not my mind."

"Then why did you go along?"

"I figured it would be better for you to find out for yourself."

Amera sighed, feeling the weight of her failure. "There's something else you should know. I'm not--"

"So why didn't you fall for it?" Curtis cut in.

"What?"

"My brother's charm. My last two assistants did."

Amera remembered the times his brother had visited his office, but although she'd found him friendly, he'd never tried to flirt with her. "I don't believe you."

"It's true," he said putting another item into the suitcase. "You can ask Owen."

Owen knew a lot. Perhaps that was why he'd seemed less than enthused about her 'holiday family' idea. She should have paid more attention. How well did she really know Kyle? She couldn't use her experience, she hadn't been the kind of woman men flirted with, although he'd always been pleasant to her. "But they haven't been married that long."

"You're right. He wasn't married then so he was free

to do what he wanted. But his behavior still annoyed me, because he had been dating Heidi for seven years by then."

Amera shook her head. "I don't know."

"You don't know what?"

"Why I never fell for him. He is very charming and was always nice to me and I thought you were..." Her words fell away.

"A bastard?"

"Yes."

"Treating my little brother unfairly?"

"Yes."

A mischievous grin touched his mouth. "And you married me anyway?"

Amera couldn't help grinning back. "Sounds like someone fishing for a compliment."

Before he could reply they heard shouting again. Curtis closed his suitcase, opened hers and started to pack it. "We're getting out of here now."

Amera helped him. "Your mother will be disappointed."

Curtis focused on packing, but his silence spoke volumes. It said 'You haven't seen drama yet.' Once he was through, he zipped up the suitcases and grabbed both. "Let's go."

"Shouldn't we say goodbye?" Amera asked, following him down the hall.

"We'll call them from the road," Curtis said.

Amera couldn't help hearing Heidi and Kyle arguing

as they made their way down the stairs and rushed towards the front door.

"I've always been faithful!" Heidi shouted.

"Really?" Kyle said. "I've been shooting blanks for three years so how did you get pregnant?"

"What?"

"I had a vasectomy."

"You lied to me. You knew I wanted another baby."

"I thought we'd agreed to just one," Kyle said.

"But you pretended to try," Heidi said in a sour tone.

"I thought you'd eventually give up on the idea."

"I went to someone else because I thought it would help us."

"That's a great story."

"It's the truth."

"Uncle Curtis!" Damon said running up to them. "You're leaving?"

"Yes," Curtis said opening the door.

"We'll see you later," Amera said in a softer tone.

"Where are you going?" an attractive older woman asked.

CHAPTER 16

Curtis swore.

The woman frowned with the condescension of a queen reprimanding a peasant. "Watch your mouth."

"Grandma's here!" Damon shouted.

"It's been a long time, Curtis." She opened her arms to hug him. He took a step back. She let her arms fall. "It's good to see you," she said. "What are you doing?"

"We're leaving," Curtis said.

Amera cleared her throat. "We have to--"

"Where are you going?" Kyle asked coming up behind them, and greeting his mother.

"They're leaving because of us, what do you think?" Heidi said, wiping her tears with her apron.

"Don't leave, we won't argue anymore," Kyle said reaching for Amera's bag. "At least stay for dinner. We have so much food."

"What's the point in stopping them? I'd leave if I could."

"Heidi, you don't mean that," Camille said.

"You don't know what he did to me."

Kyle tapped his chest. "What *I* did to you?"

Curtis set the bags down with a thud. "Not in front of your son!"

They both stared at him.

"Stop fighting in front of him. Don't think he won't remember." He glanced at his mother then looked at Damon. "It's Christmas Eve for goodness' sake. Let's make it work." He glanced at his watch then back at his brother. "You have an hour."

Kyle shook his head. "At least stay until--"

Curtis reached for his bags. "Or we can leave now."

"I'll get the dinner," Heidi said, taking Damon's hand.

"I'll finish setting the table," Kyle said then left.

Amera made a move to follow them. "I'll help you."

Curtis grabbed her hand then said in a low voice. "Stay with me."

She turned to him surprised, not by the command, but because of the slight plea she heard in his tone. She turned to his mother and held out her free hand. "It's a pleasure to meet you."

"I'm so glad both of you decided to come." His mother took off her coat and hung it up in the closet, then walked ahead of them.

Amera felt Curtis' grip on her hand tighten a fraction. "Let's go sit in the living room until dinner's ready."

Moments later the three of them sat silently in the living room. Curtis holding Amera's hand and looking everywhere, except at his mother. His mother kept glancing at him then looking away. The holiday decorations--glass angels, red ribbons and colored lights--all felt like a mockery.

"Dinner smells good," Amera said not knowing what else to say.

"Heidi is a wonderful cook," Camille said. "I'm so glad you both decided to come."

"You've already said that," Curtis said.

"Something's can't be said enough. Things like 'I'm sorry'."

He shook his head. "Let's not do this."

She clasped her hands together. "I am so sorry. Please at least let me say that."

"You've said it twice so far."

"It was so hard living with your father and I felt broken and afraid after I left him. I just wanted to forget everything."

"And me."

She waved her hands. "No. Not you."

"Do you actually think I'm going to sit here and listen to you lie to me?"

"I'm sorry." Her voice shook. "I'm sorry. You're right. When I saw you again, it was such a shock. I was just getting my life back together and I couldn't fight him. I saw you and all those fears came flooding back."

"You were drunk and angry and you blamed me for your divorce."

"It wasn't like that."

But that's all he could remember. One day, he'd taken the bus to the park near his mother's home. He'd wanted to see her, even though his father had told him she didn't want to see him. He'd known he had a half brother and sister. He saw a sad little boy with a toy car and remote sitting in his front yard. He knew the address and guessed that he was his younger brother, Kyle. He walked over to him.

"What's wrong?" he asked.

"It's broken."

He bent down, eager to help. "Let me see if I can fix it." He looked at the bottom of the toy car, opened it, altered some wires, set it on the ground then used the remote.

"It works!" Kyle said with a big grin. "Wow."

For the next fifteen minutes he played with him, showing him how to do tricks with the car.

"Can I show you my new bike?" Kyle asked.

"Sure."

"It's in the shed around back." Kyle took his hand and they started walking towards the back of the house when a voice shouted, "Kyle, where are you going?"

Curtis turned around and his heart stopped when he saw his mother. He'd last seen her when he was four years old, but had kept her memory alive through pictures. "Mom."

Her eyes widened in horror. "What are you doing here?"

"He's my new friend," Kyle said.

"Did he send you here?" Camille said in a sharp tone.

Curtis shook his head, knowing she was referring to his father.

His mother stepped closer, that's when he could smell the liquor on her. "What are you doing here?"

"I just--"

She slapped him. "You're trying to steal my son--"

"I wasn't."

She yanked Kyle away and held him tight. "You came here to steal my son! Get out of my sight."

"Camille, what's going on?" a heavy set man, her second husband, said coming out of the house.

Her tone rose with fear. "He came to take Kyle away."

Curtis shook his head, fighting back tears. "I just came to see him."

"I don't believe you."

"Honey, calm down," Mr. Carroll said. "He's just a boy."

"And he looks exactly like that damn bastard. He's his son, not mine." She pointed at him. "You stay away from my family." She turned and stumbled up the stairs with Kyle in tow. Kyle looked back at him once, his face tearstained, before his mother shoved him inside and slammed the door.

Mr. Carroll sighed. "She's been going through a lot lately. Don't take it to heart. Your mother--"

"She's not my mother," Curtis said, the pain of her rejection giving power to his words. "And I'll never be her son."

He'd gone there hoping to have a family instead of only having tutors and the house staff, but that moment killed that dream forever. Curtis looked at his mother--her grey hair in a perfect coiffure, her nails done, her brown skin lightly touched by the years--and knew he'd never see the mother he'd hoped to find.

"I never touched another drop after that day," Camille said in a soft tone. "I became a better woman."

"Congratulations." He glanced at his watch, annoyed that an hour could go by so slowly, then looked up and saw his brother staring at him in amazement.

"That was you?" Kyle said. "Sometimes I thought it was a dream. I remember you. Mom, why didn't you tell me it was him?"

"You were too young to understand," Camille said.

"You said I made it up."

"I didn't want you asking questions."

"I just remember he was my new friend and you made him leave," Kyle said.

"I wasn't myself back then."

"Why didn't you tell me?"

Her voice broke and she pulled tissues from her handbag. "Because I didn't want you to hate me too."

Kyle shook his head in regret. "God, no wonder you never wanted to see us again."

Curtis raised his brows amused. "Are you going to pity me now?"

"No."

"Then stop looking at me like that."

"I can't help it. You changed my life."

Curtis frowned. "No, I didn't."

"You made Dad see how bad Mom's drinking had gotten. She was the one who'd broken my toy. She'd tripped over it and thrown it against a wall."

Camille stood. "I'm so sorry. I'm so sorry to you both. I've regretted that moment every day since. I'd reached a new low in my life and--"

"How much do you want?" Curtis cut in.

"What?"

"Just tell me how much you want so we can get this over with and go home."

Camille shook her head. "Everything in life isn't about money."

"That's a lie people like to tell themselves," Curtis said with a sniff.

"No, that's a lie your father told you," Camille said. "He turned my heart cold and did the same to you. Life isn't about how much you have and--"

"Fifty thousand," Curtis said in a soft voice.

"What?"

"Fifty thousand," he repeated slowly.

Her eyes widened. "How did you know about that?"

"You think dear old dad would forget to tell me about that?"

"What is he talking about?" Kyle asked.

"It was more complicated than that," Camille said.

"No, it was pretty clear cut," Curtis said. "That's why you were so afraid when I showed up. You didn't want to risk your money."

"What is he talking about?" Kyle repeated.

Curtis looked up at his brother. "Fifty thousand is what she got every year for staying out of my life. Not only did she give up complete custody, she got an extra bonus for distance. Dad liked to reward good behavior and Mom wanted to be real good, didn't you?"

Camille shook her head. "No, I never spent a dime."

Curtis stood. "Is dinner ready yet?"

His brother blocked his past. "Please don't do this. Give Mom a chance."

"Why? Because it's Christmastime? I've lost a couple weeks of memory, not years. One day isn't going to change anything."

"But you were--"

Curtis felt his patience snap. "Forget who I was," he said with barely controlled rage. "This is who I am. You're both trying to make me out to be someone I'm not. I'm not that boy you remember. He's dead. Gone and he's never coming back. He was a figment of your imagination. And now it's time for us to go." He pushed past him.

"Then why did I see him again today making my son laugh?"

Curtis didn't move. He glanced down and saw Amera's hand gripped in his. He hadn't been able to release it and he still couldn't. He should. But she was the only one keeping him sane in this madhouse. A shield against his nephew's admiration, his brother's longing, his sister-in-law's confusion and his mother's regret. She'd gotten into his soul, into the deepest most fragile part of him.

He looked at Amera and saw her eyes brimming with

tears. "Oh god did I hurt you?" he asked, releasing her hand, afraid that he'd held it too tight.

"No."

"Then why are you crying?"

"I wanted to be adopted so badly, I ached every night. I pretended that I didn't care, but inside each passing day was like a penknife of pain. I wanted someone to choose me, to love me. I didn't care who--race, age, gender, I didn't care. I just wanted *someone* to want me. But no one ever did. I remember the looks from prospective parents as they glanced at me then passed by. I would dream of someone reaching out their hand to me and telling me that we were going home.

"I followed all the rules and was good and smart, but it didn't work. So I gave up. I didn't want to feel left out in the cold again. Rejected and tossed aside. I learned that wanting something that badly hurt too much. Sometimes it still does, and it hurts, because in quiet moments, I can still see that girl standing at the window staring out wondering Why not me? Why doesn't anybody want me?

"Curtis, as awful as things may seem, you have a family who wants you. They may have turned you away once, but not now."

"You weren't tossed aside."

Amera blinked. "I'm sorry?"

"You're using the wrong words," he said tenderly holding her gaze. "You weren't rejected or tossed aside. You're not an item or piece of junk that could be disposed of. You didn't get adopted because nobody was worthy of you."

She shook her head. "I'm not as worthy as you think. There's a lot of pain in this house and so many lies. I'd wanted to do something for you, but that's no excuse for causing you such pain. You've been lied to, but I'm the biggest liar of all. I'm not--"

He kissed her, then whispered against her lips. "No, not now."

"But--"

He kept his voice low, his gaze intense. "Whatever you have to tell me, tell me at home. Not here."

Camille touched her sleeve. "Amera, you have a home here if you want."

Kyle nodded in agreement. "It's not much, but it's something, right?"

"Is anybody still interested in dinner?" Heidi called out.

They ate, but nobody enjoyed the food. Forty minutes later, Amera and Curtis were heading home.

"What did you want this visit to be?" Curtis finally asked, breaking the silence.

Amera shook her head. "It's all silly now."

"Tell me."

"I wanted those things you mentioned."

"Sitting by the fire, cookies and all that?"

She nodded.

"Okay, then that's what we'll do."

And he made good on his word. Christmas morning he surprised her by serving breakfast in bed--Swedish pancakes with fresh strawberries and blueberries and a helping of whipped cream, before exchanging gifts. That evening after they indulged in a sumptuous seven-course meal, including chocolate truffles, they sat by the fire, eating gingerbread cookies and listening to the sound of silver bells on two large speakers.

"Two," Curtis said staring at the flame.

"Two what?" Amera asked, resting her head on his shoulder.

"I can see us with two kids."

Amera smiled. "A boy and a girl?"

He shrugged. "As long as they're healthy, I don't care."

She turned to him surprised. "Really? I thought you'd want two boys."

Curtis gripped his hand into a fist then relaxed it. "The only thing I want is to be a better father than my own."

"You will."

"How do you know?"

"Because you're already a better man."

His sharp gaze caught and held hers. "Don't lie to me."

"I'm not lying. Your father doesn't care about anyone, but you do. Even though you pretend not to." She lowered her eyes and sighed. As they sat on the couch with the lights dimmed and the fireplace aglow, Amera remembered the hotel room she'd set up for his proposal to Crystal. That evening hadn't ended well and she knew this one wouldn't either. She had to tell him the truth and face the consequences rather than have her heart broken when his memory returned. "There's something you should know--"

"Tell me tomorrow," he said then covered her mouth with his.

If only he could remember. Curtis lay in bed beside Amera, desperately searching his mind for clues. She was going to tell him the truth soon and he wanted to be ahead of her. But he couldn't move forward without knowing why the image of the umbrella haunted him. Who was the face he'd seen? He'd looked through several pictures and still nothing clicked. Why was his mind betraying him? He swore.

"Curtis?" Amera said.

"Did I wake you?"

"I wasn't asleep. What's wrong?"

He sat up. "Let me see the video of the dancing girl again."

"The dancing girl?"

"Yes, the one who gave me the beads."

"You're thinking of her now?" Amera said with a slight laugh. "We have this beautiful moment and you're thinking of her." She retrieved her cell phone then turned on the video. "Happy now?"

No. He was missing something. "Do you have more images from this place?"

"Yes, I have another video and--"

"Show me."

Amera eagerly got her tablet and showed him the video of Peale House. Curtis watched, remembering his boredom last time, but this time everything mattered--he looked at every room and every face. Then he saw him. One quick shot of a man passing through the hallway clicked. Suddenly, he knew who he'd seen that night.

CHAPTER 17

The cold feel of a gun nozzle pressed to his head was the last thing Vernon expected to have with his morning cup of coffee. He stood out back of Peale House and had been enjoying the crisp late December morning until now.

"I really don't like when people try to kill me," a dark voice said.

Vernon swallowed, holding up his hands. "I don't know--"

"Yes, you do."

He let his hands fall. "You have no proof."

"Not of that night, but I have plenty of information about you and this place, that could cost you a few years."

"What do you want?"

"Was the bullet meant for me or her?"

"Does it matter?"

"Do you think I'd ask you if it didn't?"

"It was just a warning to scare her off, nothing more. She was to stay away and nobody would get hurt."

"Tell me what's going on."

"Amera kept wanting to look at the books and that made us nervous."

"That's why the numbers didn't work," Curtis said, more to himself than to Vernon. "You've been doing some creative accounting and were afraid she'd eventually find some discrepancies. Right?"

Vernon nodded.

"Although you've been serving a large number of immigrants, and have huge donations to Peale House, you've been diverting some of the money into your pocket."

"No one is getting hurt."

Vernon felt the gun pressed harder. "Give me specifics," the voice said. "How do you do it?"

"We target individuals who've been given asylum, because we know about the money they receive as part of their relocation from the US government, and Peale House qualifies as a 'pass through' for this funding. But instead of giving the recipients all that they're entitled, we skim just forty-per-cent of the payment, because they don't know the exact amount they should get." Vernon swore. "There's so much money, why shouldn't we get our fair share? You have no idea what we've gone through."

"And you think that gives you the right to defraud your fellow man? People who came to this country just like you."

"They're not like us," Vernon said in an acid tone. "I didn't get a free handout and neither did Florence. There was no Peale House for us. They swarm over here like flies and feast off our riches."

Curtis stared at Vernon for a moment, seeing the young man his grandfather must have once been. A new immigrant who'd left his humanity back in a war torn land he'd escaped. He was a fighter, a survivor but somehow greed had eaten his soul. He remembered Amera's words referring to his father: *He doesn't care about anyone, but you do. Even though you pretend not to.* He couldn't pretend that he didn't care anymore.

"You have two days," Curtis said, putting his gun away. "If you want to disappear I won't stop you. But if I see you again, I'm taking you down."

Minutes later Curtis stood on the other side of the street and looked up at the old building, thinking of the corruption it hid. Millions of dollars made and only a trickle going to the residents inside. He'd have to do something. He pulled out the bracelet he'd kept in his pocket. Maya deserved a better future than this. He glanced up and saw her across the street. She looked at him and her face lit up when she saw the bracelet in his hand. He offered a brief smile and waved, affected by the delight on her face. Without warning she ran into the street.

She didn't see the car coming and the car didn't see her.

Dorothy Swartz knew she had no business going into the hospital chapel. She'd stopped practicing the faith of her ancestors years ago and didn't mind admitting that she liked Christmas music, although she thought the story behind it to be a cute fairy tale. However, that day something drew her to the chapel. Her sister, who was in the hospital recovering from surgery, was improving, but she needed a quiet place to rest.

She saw him the moment she entered. He was alone. A young black man, though at seventy-eight, everyone was starting to look young to her. He was large and fierce looking so she expected to sit down and ignore him. But then she spotted the look of devastation on his face and couldn't turn away. She'd felt that same devastation when her first husband had died after only three years of marriage and when family members died across Europe from atrocities some still refused to believe. She remembered the pain of loss and wanting to renounce life and how long it had taken her to fight her way back to being whole.

She sat down beside him, compassion overriding a small sense of unease. "Do you need to talk?"

He shook his head.

"Is the news bad?" she asked, relieved that he hadn't gotten angry.

"They don't think she'll survive the night," he said in a low voice, raw with pain.

"I'm very sorry."

He rested his arms on the back of the pew in front of him, his dark gaze fixated on the wall ahead. "I'm a fool."

"Why?"

He gritted his teeth. "I'm not supposed to care, it hurts too much."

"You'd be a fool if you didn't care, if you didn't love." She smiled when he looked at her with suspicion and surprise. "Yes. Cowards and fools are the ones with calluses on their hearts. Love is an act done by the courageous. Face the pain and love anyway. She may not last, but she felt your love and that is a timeless gift beyond measure."

Amera raced into the hospital waiting room, still stunned by the phone call she'd received from Florence. "How is she?" she asked when she saw her friend.

"It's not good. She's in a coma."

Amera fell into a chair then looked up and saw a familiar figure standing by the window. A chill swept through her. He looked like the Curtis of before--cold, lonely, distant. "What is he doing here?"

"He was there. He was by her side right after it happened. One of the attendants said Maya had seen him across the street and ran over to him. That's when she got hit."

What had Curtis been doing at Peale House? Was he looking to fund it as she'd hoped? She walked over to him.

"Go ahead and say it," he said before she could speak.

"Say what?"

"That it's my fault. That if I hadn't gone there she wouldn't have been hit."

Amera paused, surprised by the fierceness in his tone. "Why would I blame you?"

"Because I blame myself. Every time I try..." He shook his head. "When I was a little boy I wanted to be a superhero and save the world. But my grandfather and father taught me how foolish that was. Every time we flew in an airplane, my grandfather would point out the window and say 'See the cockroaches? You must always keep your distance from them.' I learned early keeping your distance also kept you safe. Because it didn't hurt as much. As a child I came to see that there were just too many problems. You fix one and a million others pop up and there was nothing I could do. Then or now."

"So you stopped caring."

"It was easier that way, but now I don't see cockroaches or rats anymore. I just see faces everywhere. But there's still nothing I can do."

"You already did something."

He turned to her, doubtful. "What?"

"You made her smile. You noticed her out of all the other children. All we want is for someone to say 'I see you', 'you're not alone.' I know. I wanted someone to pick me out and look at me, not glance over me, but to really see me and you did that for Maya. Florence told me how she was planning a new dance, just in case I came and visited again."

"Is that supposed to matter?"

"Yes, you made her happy and that's priceless."

"I now understand your story about the two bakers," he said with a tired sigh. "I just met a woman who told me something I'd never heard before." He returned his gaze to the window. "I'm not the man I used to be, Em."

Em! He hadn't called her that in days. Had his memory returned so quickly and without warning? "Are you feeling okay?" she asked cautious.

He kept his gaze focused outside. "You want to know if my memory's back?"

She nodded.

"Yes, it is."

"Completely?"

"Yes."

She wrung her hands then let them fall, apprehension sweeping through her. "So you remember that night and the days afterwards?"

"Every moment."

Her heart thudded in her chest, she'd been fearing this day. "You must have a lot of questions."

"Right now, just one," he said. He turned to her, his dark gaze capturing hers. "Will you marry me for real?"

CHAPTER 19

She didn't know how to respond. Wasn't he supposed to be angry? Had he really changed so much?

"Em?"

"Are you sure your memory's back?"

He nodded.

"When?"

He folded his arms. "You're actually going to make me wait for an answer?"

She rubbed her head. "I don't understand."

"I'm asking you to marry me for real."

She stared at him stunned. "For real?"

He grinned. "Yes, my little parrot. For real."

"But I pretended to be your wife."

"Yes, and talked to me about why I should keep Valdan open, and fund Peale House and helped me see my family for who they are."

Amera licked her lip. "And you're not angry?".

"No."

"Why not?"

"Because I'm in love with you."

Amera stared at him, torn by conflicting emotions. Joy and fear and sorrow. She had no right to feel this happy when little Maya was dying. She swallowed hard and bit back tears. "Why were you at Peale House?"

He glanced at Florence, then back at Amera. "I can't tell you that right now."

"I need to know." She needed time to think, to digest the man he'd become.

"I found out some information I needed to verify."

"What information?"

"Peale House has been defrauding people," he said keeping his voice low so no one could overhear them. "That's why I didn't like their numbers. They're fake."

"You must be mistaken. Florence is--"

"I'm not mistaken. Vernon tried--" He bit his lip then started again. "I spoke to Vernon and he confirmed what I suspected. I want you to stay away from there."

His words didn't make sense. Florence was warm and caring and they shared the same hopes for Peale House. Didn't they? "But I saw the proposal and--"

"Do you trust me?"

Amera hesitated, stunned by the iron in his tone. Curtis didn't waste his time on things that didn't matter to him. She sighed with weariness, feeling the sadness of losing a friendship. "Yes."

"Then do as I say and stay away."

"What about the families and the workers and--"

"I'm already looking into things."

Amera briefly closed her eyes, feeling foolish. "How could I have been so blind?"

Curtis shoved his hands into his pockets and stared back out the window. "Are you really not going to answer me, Em?"

"Yes."

His jaw twitched but he nodded. "Okay, I accept that."

She playfully nudged him with her elbow. "I mean the answer is yes."

He turned to her surprised. "Really?"

She grinned. "Yes my little parrot. Really."

He continued to stare at her, dumbfounded.

She laughed at his expression, joy replacing some of the sadness in her heart. "Did you really expect me to say no?"

"I don't know what I expected." He grabbed her hand and held it against his heart. "If Maya survives, I want us to adopt her."

Amera looked into his intense gaze, her heart fluttered wildly in her chest. At that moment she'd say yes to anything. "Okay."

He gathered her into his arms and whispered. "I'll make you happy, Em."

Amera buried her face in his neck, for once believing in magic and that anything was possible.

❄

"That's not going to happen."

Curtis tapped a finger against the foot of his father's bed. "I didn't come here to ask your permission," he said, careful to keep his tone neutral. "I've made my choice."

His father flashed a cruel smile. "You trying to grow a backbone or something?"

"I have never asked you for anything--"

"Why start now? Forget her. It's not going to happen."

"She--"

"She has no history, no background, no money. Nothing that will benefit us. Her bloodline could be tainted."

"I don't care--"

"Come here."

Curtis gripped his hand into a fist. "Father."

"Come here."

He reluctantly did.

Bishop Senior grabbed his shirt and slapped him with the back of his hand. "Marry her and I'll close Valdan for good within the month. I heard you've gotten attached to it."

"Those people depend on their jobs and their families--"

"Have you given the rats names too?"

"They're not rats."

"They are whatever I say they are." He shoved him away in disgust then smoothed out a wrinkle in his duvet. "I'm not an unreasonable man, but I'm not a generous one either. I don't think it's a hard choice." He rested his head back and closed his eyes. "You either care for your rats or you don't."

Curtis stared at his father, knowing he'd been dismissed but unable to leave. He wanted to strike him. To make him see reason, but he knew he never would. He didn't mind the slaps or the insults. He'd grown used to them, but he could no longer see others hurt because of him.

He left his father's house and sat in his car, his mind searching for the right strategy. It was an impossible choice. Hundreds of people could lose their jobs because of his selfish desire to be with the woman he loved. But the thought of living without her was unbearable. He took out the bracelet he kept with him. Maya was still in a coma, but at times he imagined seeing her smiling at him or dancing. He imagined having a conversation with her and placed the bracelet on the seat where Amera usually sat.

"What should I do?" he asked.

"You should do good," Maya replied with childlike innocence.

"Doing good is hard."

"Why?" Maya asked.

"Because I never thought about it before."

"Being a good person is better than being a bad person, right?"

Sometimes I wonder, he muttered as the image of Maya disappeared. He thought of Jorge who'd pleaded for leniency for his sister; Maria's finely woven shirts; her little boy who'd nearly lost his hand because his mother had taken him to work; Bill who had once saved Amera's life and now faced joblessness. All of them had lives and families. He had nothing. He didn't have anything to lose. "She never said she loved me," he whispered to himself, ashamed at the tightening of his throat and the brief stinging of tears. If she had said those words, it would have been harder to let her go, but she hadn't. His life would remain as it always had been--separate and distant from the rest.

He'd make her hate him, that would be the easiest way to let her go.

Amera looked at Miranda stunned. "I'm being what?"

"Transferred," Miranda said, nervously toying with her necklace. "With a generous raise in pay I might add," she said with a bright smile.

"Excuse me." Amera marched into Curtis' office unannounced. "You have to talk to HR," she said walking up to his desk. "There's been a mistake."

Curtis kept his gaze on his computer screen. "There's no mistake."

"You're having me transferred?"

"I believe it's for the best."

Amera shook her head, perplexed. "If you didn't want me to work here after we get married you could have just told me."

He rubbed his chin. "That was a mistake. I made a hasty decision."

She stared at him confused. "You think the proposal was a mistake?"

"We were both over emotional at the hospital and--"

"I wasn't. My answer was real."

He lifted his gaze to hers. "My question wasn't. It was a moment of brief desperation. I'm sorry I involved you."

Amera leaned forward, resting her hands on his desk, anger surging through her. "I should have known it was too good to be true, that you would seek revenge somehow. When did you decide to get back at me?"

"This has nothing to do with--"

"Were your promises to Valdan and Bill lies too? Did you make up that story about Peale House just to hurt me?"

"No, those were real."

"Am I supposed to believe that? Maybe I should go to Florence and find out for myself."

Curtis surged to his feet. "I said stay away from there and I meant it."

"Of course," Amera scoffed. "I'm supposed to trust you."

His eyes bore into hers. "Yes."

"So only your feelings for me were fake. I see." She spotted Maya's bracelet on his desk and reached for it.

He grabbed her wrist. "Leave it."

Tears sprung to her eyes, wounded by the strength of emotion behind his words. He felt more for this child than he had for her. He made her feel like an overlooked orphan again--bereft and desolate. She'd been foolish to think she'd have a home with him. She hated him for letting her taste the sweetness of having a dream come true before ripping it away. She yanked her wrist free and stepped back. "All right."

"Keep the ring and forget about me. I'll have all your clothes delivered to your place." When she didn't move he lifted a brow in derision. "Are you waiting to see my nosebleed? You'll be disappointed."

Amera snatched the bracelet before he could stop her and broke it in two, sending beads flying everywhere. She delighted in the pain that briefly swept crossed his face. *Now you know how it feels you bastard,* her heart screamed. But she held his gaze, letting her tears dry and said in a cool voice. "I'll send you a check."

The moment she left, Curtis fell to his knees and gathered every last bead he could find. It was a frenzied effort that allowed him not to think. Not to think about how easily Amera had ripped his heart as she had the bracelet. He felt as scattered as the beads--lost, vulnerable, small and he hated the feeling. Not once had she said she loved him, even after he'd made his declaration plain. And that realization sent a fresh new anguish searing through his heart.

Has she gotten you on your knees now? He could hear his father mocking him. *Look at how pathetic you've become.* But even with his father's cruel words echoing in his mind, he couldn't stop picking up the beads, thinking of how he would restring the bracelet. He'd gathered most of them when he heard a knock on the door.

"Come in," he said.

Owen entered. "What are you doing?"

"What does it look like I'm doing?" Curtis snapped, picking up another bead and putting it in his hand. "Watch your step."

"Um..."

He looked up at him annoyed. "What?"

Owen pointed at him then gestured to his own face. Curtis sniffed then rubbed his nose and saw the blood. He swore. If Amera had waited a minute longer she would have seen his weakness, he was relieved she hadn't. He grabbed a tissue then looked at the beads he'd been able to gather. He gazed at them with a sense of shame instead of triumph. What the hell had he been trying to do? How could he try to fix what was irrevocably broken? He'd been gathering up the tiny beads like a madman. But he had to be practical. Maya and Amera would no longer be part of his life. He'd made his choice and had to be man enough to stand by it. He dumped the beads in the trashcan and sat behind his desk.

"What do you want?"

"I got the information you wanted on Vernon, Florence and Peale House," Owen said.

"Good. Now find someone to make sure Amera stays away from there."

"I heard Amera's being transferred. Are you still keeping your relationship a secret?"

"There is no relationship," Curtis said, checking messages on his phone.

Owen squeezed his eyes shut and pinched the bridge of his nose. "I don't understand you two. You're perfect together and she loves you and you love her."

Curtis' head shot up. "Did she say that?"

"Say what?"

"That she loves me?"

"No, but--"

Curtis returned his gaze to his phone and said in a velvet voice of warning, "Then shut up and never mention that again."

CHAPTER 20

$\mathcal{A}$mera called Florence for the tenth time, wondering why her friend wouldn't answer. She'd left her messages and sent her texts and emails and gotten no reply. She hadn't spoken to her since she'd last seen her at the hospital several days ago. She refused to believe what Curtis had told her about Peale House. Florence was a kind person and had suffered so much, she wouldn't use her position as a means to defraud people. Curtis was just a vindictive bastard who didn't care. No, that was wrong. He did care, he cared about a little girl, but not her. She'd never mattered to him.

Amera drove to Peale House, briefly thinking of Curtis' warning before brushing it aside. He had no right to tell her anything. She heard the sirens before she saw them. Amera drove up to the building and found it surrounded by police and an ambulance. She saw a stretcher being carried away into a van from the morgue.

She parked and jumped out and saw Florence in tears. She ran up to her.

"What happened?"

Florence spun around with a mask of rage. "Why couldn't you stay away?"

"What?"

"You killed him!" She lunged at Amera, scratching and punching her face before pulling her hair and biting her arm. Amera fought back but she was no match to Florence's fury and it took three police officers to pull her away.

Amera put a hand to her bleeding face and stared at her friend confused. "Florence--"

"He wouldn't have done this if not for you. He was good to me. But he couldn't take it anymore. He put the gun to his head but you killed him!"

Amera could only stare at Florence as the officers dragged her away and put her in a cruiser. One of the EMTs approached Amera, offering assistance, but she waved him away.

"I told you to stay away from here."

Amera froze at the sound of Curtis' voice. He was the last person she wanted to see. She turned and headed to her car.

He grabbed her arm and spun her around to face him. He swore when he saw the bruises and scratches. "Em I--"

She slapped him with such force that her hand stung from the impact. "Don't ever touch me or call me that again."

"He took the coward's way out."

"What?"

"He didn't want to face his crimes and didn't have the fight to run from them so he left Florence to clean up his mess. She's going to need a very good lawyer. Fortunately, I have enough connections to keep Peale House going while we restructure everything. I've hired a new director and some more employees so--"

"How much profit?"

He blinked. "There's no profit."

"In your hands you'll turn it into one, right? That's what you bastards are good at."

He nodded. "You're right," he said, releasing her then walked away.

Amera stared at his back for a long moment then turned and walked in the opposite direction. She didn't know how far she walked before the tears began to fall. She'd never seen such hate on Florence's face before. She couldn't believe that Curtis had been right about them.

She couldn't trust people. Florence had betrayed her and she should never have opened her heart to Curtis. She'd broken her rules and suffered for it. But she wouldn't again.

She remembered the pain she felt when her clothes from Curtis' place arrived at her door. But she fought her sadness with an iron will. She was determined not to be unhappy. She would never be vulnerable again. She didn't understand people and all she saw was that they hurt each other. Just like Curtis' mother hurt her son, Kyle hurt his wife and she hurt him in return, and

Florence hurt her. People weren't meant to be trusted. Fleeting foolish love was all one could hope for and she'd tasted it and found it bitter.

She thought about the Black Stockings Society. She'd gotten to live a little dangerously and gotten a great wardrobe out of it. But their guarantee of love had been a false claim. She didn't blame them. She blamed herself for believing them. Curtis had made his way in this world by not caring and she would too. He hadn't been fooled by Peale House like she had. He kept himself distant and kept himself safe. She would follow his example and focus only on building her career.

She pulled out her phone when it buzzed and saw a text from Owen.

Where are you going?

It was a strange question. How would he know she was going somewhere? Unless...She looked around then saw Owen waving from his car behind her.

She walked up to him. "What are you doing?"

"Following Bishop's orders. He told us to look out for you."

"Us?"

"Never mind. Forget I said that." He opened the passenger side. "Let me drive you back to your car."

"I can walk."

"It's a long walk. Several miles in fact."

She paused. "Miles?"

He nodded.

Amera sighed, suddenly feeling weary without her anger to fuel her. "Okay," she said getting inside.

"Do you want to stop by the hospital?" he asked pulling from the curb.

"No."

"Bishop told me about the little girl from Peale House, Margaret."

"Maya."

"Yeah, Maya. She's awake now, but she'll never walk again."

A heavy feeling settled in her stomach and she felt as cold as the late December day. Maya would never dance again and create the magic she loved. Amera thought of going to see her, then decided to stay away. She had nothing to offer the little girl. She privately hated how she only thought of Maya with pain and a tinge of jealousy. She'd been jealous that although she'd tucked Maya into bed, the little girl had offered Curtis the present, not her. And although she'd played his wife and helped him through a difficult time, in the end Curtis had held onto Maya's gift, and offered to adopt her and let Amera go. Even under false pretense, to others she'd still remained invisible. Why didn't anyone remember her? Make her feel that what she gave was important? He'd said he loved her then withdrawn what he had said so quickly to cling onto a string of plastic beads.

Amera tugged on the ring on her finger, surprised to feel it move, when it hadn't so much as budged before, then she pulled it off. She held it out to Owen. "Here."

He glanced at the ring then looked back at the road. "What?"

"I want you to have it."

"What would I do with a ring like that?"

"Lots of things. If you're a true romantic you can give it to the woman you plan to marry some day."

"If I give her something like that, she'll think I'm rich."

Amera stuffed it in his coat pocket. "Then sell it."

He took the ring out of his pocket. "Bishop would kill me."

"Stop exaggerating."

"I'm not. Some people don't think Vernon's death was really a suicide. That bastard's capable of anything."

"He's not capable of that."

"How do you know? The Bishops can make something happen with just a phone call."

Amera rolled her eyes, angered by the assumption. "I know Curtis. He may be a lot of things, but he's not a killer. You're just saying that to annoy me."

Owen shook his head and set the ring on her lap. "No, I said it to see how much you still care."

Camille sat in her conservatory finishing lunch with Kyle, as a hazy January sun hung in the sky, amazed by how much had changed in a few weeks. He and Heidi were working on their marriage and Damon had become less destructive. She still wished she'd had a chance to talk with Curtis more, but had been glad she'd at least been able to see him, although she knew it was probably the last time. Her assistant bustled into the room. "Um..your son is on the phone."

"My son?" She looked at Kyle. "He's right here."

"No, the other one."

Camille sat up stunned. Curtis was on the phone? She took a deep steadying breath then answered. "Hello."

"I forgive you," he said with such sincerity it brought tears to her eyes. "I understand that you had to make a choice."

"I regretted it."

"Don't. You did what you thought was best."

The weariness in his tone alerted her that something was wrong. "What has the bastard done?"

Curtis laughed without humor. "What a bastard always does."

"If he forces you to make a choice you have to ignore it."

"It's too late."

"It's never too late." She hated to hear her son in pain, but there was nothing she could do. They were still strangers. But if she couldn't be his mother, she could be his guide. "It won't be easy, but regret is a torturous monster. Your father believes in black or white, winners or losers. But the world has many gray areas and that's where the wise and happy reside. It's called compromise."

"You know he won't," Curtis said.

"Exactly, so you must change the rules and play a new game. A game you can win."

"And if I fail?"

Camille shook her head. "If you fear failure you've already lost."

He hesitated. "It's too late. Even when I win, I lose."

She was almost done. Amera looked at her bags full of clothes ready for donation with pride. She would never go to another party and most of the outfits would go to waste in her closet, clearing them out was the best thing to do. She had handed in her resignation, but wasn't concerned about getting another position. She already had two interviews lined up for next week. She'd set some items aside to give to Susan whose calls she'd been ignoring for the last week. She didn't want to lose her as a friend, but couldn't talk to anyone right now. She placed the bags near the door and was about to turn on the TV when the doorbell rang.

She opened it and saw a woman who looked familiar. "Hello?"

"You haven't worn your last pair yet," she said.

Amera frowned confused. "I'm sorry?"

The woman held out her hand. "I'm Rania."

Amera nodded now remembering her face from the video message she'd received from the Black Stockings Society. "A pleasure."

Rania walked in and sat down. "Why haven't you worn your last pair yet?"

"I didn't realize I was on a time schedule."

"So you were planning on wearing them later?"

"Yes. Would you like something to drink?"

"When?" Rania asked, ignoring her question.

"I don't know. Does it matter?" Amera said taking a seat in front of her.

"Do you think I'm here to amuse myself? I always know when a member is about to give up."

"I haven't given up anything."

"Really?" Rania crossed her legs then pointed to the bags of clothing in the corner. "Then what are those doing there?"

"Just a donation."

"You just got new clothes how come you're getting rid of them so soon?"

Amera shrugged. "I won't have use for them any time in the future."

"How do you know?"

"I just do."

Rania nodded slowly, as if trying to comprehend Amera's words. "So you *don't* know when you'll wear your last pair of stockings, but you *do* know you'll never need beautiful clothes for a night out again."

"Yes."

Rania smiled. "You're a cool one. You're not even upset."

"There's no reason to be."

"Didn't we promise you a new love life? We guaranteed it."

Amera sat back and folded her arms, amused. "Marketing is another form of storytelling and we know that most stories are usually false."

"Then why did you believe him?"

She stiffened. "Who?"

"Curtis. Why did you believe the story he told you?"

"He didn't tell me a story."

"Then why aren't you with him?"

Amera sat up and let her hands fall to her sides. "Because he said that asking me to marry him was a mistake. He'd made a hasty decision."

"And you believed him."

"Of course."

"Why?"

"Because that was the truth."

"How do you know?"

"I just do."

Rania shook her head. "That's not like you, Amera. You like to deal with facts and figures. You listened with your heart that day, but didn't listen to his words. Because the truth is, Curtis is not a man who makes hasty decisions. But you *chose* to believe that anyway. Why?" She stood and spoke before Amera could. "I'll tell you why, because the truth sounded like a story to you. Something too good to be true. How could he really love you? How could he really want to have a family with you? So you chose the lie instead."

"He told me--"

"How many times has he said things he doesn't mean, because he has to? Why didn't you wait for a nosebleed." Rania's grin grew at Amera's shock. "Yes, I have spies. We know a lot about you two."

"We?"

"The Society."

Amera stood ready to show her the door. "Well, you don't have to look after me anymore."

"Our work isn't done yet."

"I don't care."

Rania's grin disappeared. "It's dangerous not to care."

"It's smarter that way. I don't care if Curtis did or didn't love me, whether Peale House succeeds or fails, whether Maya walks or doesn't. They have nothing to do with me. I'm living my own life and everyone is living theirs."

"Then I guess we made a mistake with you. Just like you never got adopted, you shouldn't have been invited into our exclusive club."

Amera gasped as if she'd been slapped, Rania's words ripping open a tender wound. Tears choked her throat. "I deserved to get adopted. It's that no one good enough came by."

"Who said that?"

"Cur--" She stopped and bit her lip.

"Who?

"Curtis," she whispered, reluctantly remembering the strength his words had given her.

"Funny you should quote him."

Amera pointed at her. "You can laugh at me. Just don't say I don't deserve the membership because I do."

"How do you know that? You don't even know the requirements."

"Why are you saying these things?"

"Why do you care?" Rania said, picking up one of the bags and placing it on the couch. "Amera, you hide then blame people for not seeing you."

"That's not true."

Rania pulled a blouse out of the bag. "Tell me about Maya."

"She's a little girl I met at Peale House. Curtis pointed her out and I asked her to dance."

"For you?"

"No, for him."

Rania took out another blouse and set it aside. "Why didn't you ask her to dance for you?"

"I don't know," Amera said, perplexed by the other woman's behavior and questions. "I just thought it would be better."

"So you hid behind Curtis to get her to dance."

Amera frowned. "That's not--"

"And when did you tell Curtis that you loved him?"

Amera sat down and motioned to one of the tops. "Take as much as you want."

"You didn't tell him did you?"

Amera stood and grabbed another bag. "Since you're here you can take them all."

Rania pulled out a scarf, impressed. "Gorgeous color." She set the scarf down. "So he didn't say I love you first?"

"He didn't mean it."

"So he *did* say it?"

"I told you. It was a hasty decision he regretted. I'm glad I didn't say I loved him back, that would have been worse. He's the one who changed his mind. He didn't really love me. He didn't come back to me. He wants to adopt Maya instead."

Rania sent her a sharp look. "Instead? Did you expect him to adopt you too? Are you a child?"

Amera waved her hand. "That was a slip of the tongue."

"No, it wasn't," Rania said, pinning her with a hard look. "You're still so worried about being picked that you don't realize how powerful you are."

"Powerful? Me?"

"Yes. Why didn't you pick Maya out as special? Why

didn't you pick Curtis to be the man you would love? You keep waiting, like in the stories, to be the chosen one, but in real life many times you have to pick yourself and that's when life truly begins. You take the lead and say 'I will love you' 'I'm amazing and deserve happiness.' 'I will care about you'. Not 'Will you care about me and make me happy?' If you'd truly loved Curtis, you would have waited for the truth or uncovered it on your own because you would have known that whether he loved you or not, you deserve to be loved."

Amera folded her arms tight. "Love hurts too much. It's better to stay away."

"No, Amera. You've grown too used to pain and I'm here to tell you it's time to welcome joy. Stop avoiding Susan because you think she has the life you never will. Stop imaging that your future will be the same as your past. Remember the Black Stockings oath?"

"No."

Rania sighed, tapped something into her phone then held the phone out to Amera. "Read it out loud."

"As a member of the Black Stockings Society I swear I will not reveal club secrets, I will accept nothing but the best and I will no longer settle for less."

Rania nodded. "You're not supposed to settle. I want you to put all your clothes back in the closet and wear your last pair of stockings within the next two weeks."

That didn't sound too hard. "That's all?"

"No, I want you to wear the stockings to the factory and tell Bill the truth. Isn't it time you let go of your first love?"

How foolish it seemed now to have had an unrequited love for so long. He'd been a young doctor in his early thirties when he'd come into her life. She'd given him drawings and written stories and left sweets on his desk in the clinic. She'd desperately wanted him to like her and see her and take her away. But he'd chosen someone else instead. Someone else who'd needed him more. A young boy with albinism, whose tender skin was scoured by the heat and whose light eyes were legally blinded by the sun. A young boy who she'd spent many days reading stories to and who'd imagined the touch of ice and snow along with her.

Before going to the factory, Amera decided to dress her best, wearing a moderately short, red linen skirt, to show off her stockings. They were black silk stockings, with a contrasting red seam down the back, and silk-screened image of a rose on each ankle. She selected a fitted, short-sleeved cashmere top, in soft pink, and accentuated the look with a thin, brown patent leather belt. To finish off the look, Amera added a stunning pair of diametrically designed, silver hoops, then pulled her hair back, and up, leaving it just a little unruly, to add a sense of danger.

Amera knocked on Bill's office door.

He opened it and stared at her then his face spread into a wide smile. "I don't know what you did, but you did it. He's a changed man. I don't know how to thank you. You said you'd find a way to keep the factory open and you did."

"I did?"

He ushered her inside. "Don't be coy. I just got word from Bishop that the factory is safe. But aside from that he's made the morale here increase twofold by discussing child care options."

"Actually I didn't come here to talk about him," Amera said taking a seat.

"Oh," Bill said closing the door. He sat opposite her. "What is it?"

She pulled out a worn photograph of her in the hospital with Bill, both smiling at the camera. "Many years ago, you saved my life--"

He snatched the picture from her and stared at it amazed. "I don't believe it. For so many years I didn't feel as if I made a difference." He lifted his watery gaze to hers. "This little girl was you?"

"Yes."

He closed his eyes. "I remember the scent of coconut oil and aloe. Children singing and the sounds of a soccer ball bouncing on the dirt." He glanced down at the photo. "And I remember this odd little girl with a serious face, light hair and eyes."

Amera's heart leaped. He remembered her, at least that was something. "I wanted to thank you."

"You don't have to thank me. I did what I went there to do."

"But you didn't have to adopt my brother."

He looked at her startled. "Your brother?"

"Yes, my brother was a couple years younger than me."

He shook his head. "No one told me there were two of you. I wouldn't have separated you if--"

"It was for the best. The director wanted to keep it a secret in case you thought you had to take me too and she didn't want to ruin my brother's chances."

"No," he said fiercely. "They should have told me I would have taken you too."

"Really?"

"Of course. I'd mentioned adopting another child, but the director said a single guy like me would be better off with just one child. She said a child with his condition would need special care. And at the time he was really sick. My god, I didn't even think to question why I let her persuade me out of it. I'm so sorry."

Amera flung her arms around him, her heart singing. Someone had cared. Someone had seen her. Someone had wanted her, even briefly. And not just someone. Him. "Thank you," she said drawing away, not ashamed by the depth of her feelings for him.

"For what?"

"Even considering it."

He leaned against his desk. "It's like I've won the lottery or something. First the factory not closing, then my older son--your brother--won a scholarship he didn't even remember applying for. He'd had to delay his schooling and help me when things got tight, but I'd always promised him that he'd be able to finish his degree, now he can. And my younger son was selected by a special needs program all expenses paid. Now this."

For a moment Amera couldn't breathe. Curtis had kept his promise. Why? He didn't have to. It didn't make sense. "I have to go."

"Wait, you can't just leave like this."

"I'll call you," she said giving him one last hug before leaving.

Amera stumbled to her car as if in a fog. Curtis hadn't lied about Peale House being crooked, he'd kept Valdan functioning and he'd helped Bill. Why had he done all that but coldly withdrawn his proposal? Was Rania right? Was there something more behind what he had said? She didn't want to care, she didn't want to love him, but she did.

She sat in her car and drummed her fingers on the steering wheel. Something about Bill's words kept echoing in her mind. Bishop said the factory is safe. Not that it had a reprieve, but safe. How had he managed that? She knew Bishop Senior.... Amera rested her hand on the steering wheel as a realization struck her. She'd never thought about his father. She'd forgotten the power he had. No doubt Bishop Senior had something to do with Curtis changing his mind. Of course he'd never let her know. He'd prefer to push her away.

Amera pounded the steering wheel. "Curtis you bastard," she said, remembering the look of pain that had crossed his face when she'd ripped Maya's bracelet. "What have you done?" Amera put her keys in the ignition, determined to find out.

CHAPTER 22

"Did you shake hands with the devil?"

Curtis froze at the sound of her voice. It was the last thing he expected to hear on his drive home from the office. He'd gotten into his car after a long day at work, never paying attention to who was at the wheel. "What are you doing?"

"Driving you home, sir. That's what we cockroaches do. Or am I a rat?"

Curtis gripped his hands into fists. "Stop it, Em."

"You don't have to give me a nickname, sir. I know I don't mean anything to you, but thanks for what you did for Bill."

Curtis shifted his gaze to the traffic.

"He told me that the factory is safe. How did you do that?"

Curtis tapped the window with the back of his fingers. "You never used to talk this much."

"I never used to love you this much either."

His fingers stopped. "Pull over."

"No."

He met her gaze in the rearview mirror. "Why are you doing this?"

"Have you ever thought of hiring me as your driver? I could use the work."

"Stop it, Em."

"Your father doesn't have to know."

"I said pull over," he said in a firm voice.

"No."

"How can you be my driver when you can't even follow directions?"

"I'll pull over in two minutes."

He unlocked the door and started to open it.

Amera looked back at him in alarm. "Are you crazy?"

"Either you pull over or I get out now."

Amera swore then pulled over to the side and parked. "I just wanted to--"

Curtis jumped out of the car and slammed the door before she could finish.

She sighed and hung her head in defeat. He'd won again. She looked up when he knocked on the window. When she didn't move, he motioned for her to get out.

She pushed the car door open and reluctantly rose to her feet. "Curtis--."

His gaze drifted down from her hat to her stockings. "What kind of driver are you supposed to be?"

"A tempting one."

His gaze heated. "You've succeeded."

She reached for his collar and pulled him close.

He shook his head. "But I'm not kissing you."

She grinned. "Right, I'm kissing you."

He shook his head again. "You're not doing that either."

Her smile fell and she searched his face suddenly unsure. "Why not? Don't you--"

He pressed a finger against her lips, his dark gaze hard. "Em, I'm the son of a bastard. There are few things I fear and my father--"

Amera removed his hand. "Will never let you forget your failures. Every great man has failures. But truly great men have families and friends. People who care about them and that's something your father has never had, but you do. You don't have to live in the shadow of the Bishops anymore. You don't have to do it the way it's always been done and you don't have to stay under your father's grip the rest of your life. Stop waiting for him to die so that you can be free."

He drew her close and held her. "I'm so tired," he said with a deep raspy sigh. "Every day without you has been...like I was cast out of heaven." He shook his head. "I don't want to lose you again."

She cupped his face then kissed him. "What would people say if they knew you were a man of such sweet words?"

"It would ruin my reputation."

"I think that would do my fiancé some good."

The corner of his mouth kicked up in a grin. "I'm listening."

The bastard still wasn't dead, but the machines at Valdan hummed as normal. The workers didn't care that Benjamin Marshall Bishop continued to rule his empire from his sick bed. Or that his son Curtis Bishop was the spitting image of his father, tall and dark, with ruggedly handsome features. When he suddenly appeared that Monday morning after the Thanksgiving holiday and stood high above the factory floor casting his gaze over the workers, the hum of the machines slowly came to a stop quickly replaced by the sound of applause and celebration.

Curtis took the microphone Bill had handed him and motioned for them to stop. In a shrewd deal he'd wrestled control of the factory from his father's company and gone out on his own. Using Maria's design he'd established a specialized clothing line and garnered deals with two other companies. She and Jorge would never have to worry about money again.

"It's good to be here," Curtis said when they finally quieted down.

"When's the baby due?" one of the workers shouted.

Curtis grinned and looked over at his wife, Amera, who was five months along. "In the spring. We don't know if Maya will get a little brother or sister." He said casting his glance at the beaming little girl who sat in a wheelchair by his side. "But I'm not here because of my family. I'm here because of you. My second family."

They erupted in cheers again.

"We did so well this year, we can afford to shut the factory down for a week so you can spend time with your families. Happy Holidays."

The crowd shouted their thanks and love.

"Are you sure that isn't too generous?" Bill asked, his voice barely heard above the shouts.

Curtis just sent him a look and Bill knew it wise not to argue.

"Can I have two minutes?" Amera asked.

Curtis glanced at her then Bill. "One," he said then took Maya's wheelchair and left.

"Will we be seeing you for dinner?" Amera asked.

"Of course."

The year before she'd reunited with her brother and grown close with Bill's family. Kyle and Heidi had worked on their marriage and welcomed another boy into their family. Camille was back in her son's life and slowly rebuilding his trust. She'd helped Curtis and Amera set up Maya's room.

Amera walked to the car inhaling the scent of ever-greens before getting inside.

"I forgot to give you this," Curtis said pulling a box out of his coat pocket. "Susan stopped by and said she couldn't make our dinner this year, but wanted you to have this."

Amera opened the box, curious since they hadn't agreed to exchange gifts. Susan had already given her a gift that couldn't be wrapped. A friendship she'd always treasure. She opened the box and saw a crystal angel inside. The one she'd wanted to buy at the gift shop.

"Mommy, why are you crying?" Maya asked worried.

Amera brushed away her tears and looked at Maya then Curtis with such love she wasn't sure her heart could take it. "I never thought I could be this happy."

Curtis handed her a tissue, his eyes melting into hers. Reflected in his dark brown gaze she saw a man who loved her. A man who'd helped her build the family she'd always wanted. She'd seen him encourage Maya through every labored step in physical therapy and felt the strength of his embrace as he spun her in delight when they'd learned they were expecting. She knew defying his father had been hard, but they'd weathered the storm together. She dabbed her eyes then looked at the tissue, a realization hitting her. "You haven't had to use these lately."

"What?"

She waved the tissue in a gesture of triumph. His nosebleeds were gone. "You haven't had to use these in over a year."

He winked. "I know."

Maya held out her hands and wiggled her fingers with childish eagerness. "Can I see what's in the box?"

Amera placed the angel in her hands. "Be careful," she said then she looked down at the box and saw a note card tucked under the tissue. "I told you it was never too late for love," it read. But it wasn't the words that made her gasp and then laugh. It was the shape of them. Susan had formed the words in the shape of a stocking.

ABOUT THE AUTHOR

Dara Girard, an award-winning, national bestselling author of more than forty novels, from romance to suspense, loves telling stories.

Born in the US to immigrant parents, Dara enjoys pulling from her Jamaican, British, Nigerian heritage and exposure to various cultures to bring what reviewers and fans call "vivid emotional stories" to life. She is best known for her popular Henson Series, the mysterious Clifton Sisters, and the fun Black Stockings Society.

You can write her at:

contactdara@daragirard.com

or

P.O. Box 10345

Silver Spring, MD 20914

If you'd like to receive a reply, please send a self-addressed stamped envelope.

Visit her website to sign up for her newsletter and get sneak peeks, monthly updates on new releases, and special offers.

For more information visit
www.daragirard.com